— AKIMA'S STORY —

— AKIMA'S STORY —

A Novel by
KEVIN J. ANDERSON &
REBECCA MOESTA

▲
ACE BOOKS, NEW YORK

TITAN A.E.™: AKIMA'S STORY

An Ace Book / published by arrangement with
Twentieth Century Fox Animation

PRINTING HISTORY
Ace edition / May 2000

The Penguin Putnam Inc. World Wide Web site address is
http://www.penguinputnam.com

Check out the Ace Science Fiction & Fantasy newsletter
and much more on the Internet at Club PPI!

ISBN: 0-441-00738-4

ACE®
Ace Books are published
by The Berkley Publishing Group,
a division of Penguin Putnam Inc.,
375 Hudson Street, New York, New York 10014.
ACE and the "A" design are trademarks
belonging to Penguin Putnam Inc.

PRINTED IN THE UNITED STATES OF AMERICA

10 9 8 7 6 5 4 3 2 1

— ACKNOWLEDGMENTS —

Special thanks to many special people.

Ginjer Buchanan from Ace Books: for choosing to work with us on yet another fun book project.

Virginia King, Melissa Cobb, and Jennifer Robinson from Fox: for your faith in us, and for listening to our ideas.

Matt Bialer of the William Morris Agency: for convincing us this would be an entertaining and worthwhile project.

Catherine Sidor and Diane Davis Herdt from WordFire, Inc.: for all the hours and effort you put in to help us finish this book and make it as good as it could be.

Jonathan MacGregor Cowan: for putting up with weeks and months of "Not right now." "Can it wait?" "I'm almost done." And so on.

— ABOUT THE AUTHORS —

Kevin J. Anderson and Rebecca Moesta (a husband-and-wife team) have written two dozen books together, and dozens more separately. For more information on their works, please visit them on the Web at www.wordfire.com or www.dunenovels.com, or write to them care of

AnderZone
P.O. Box 767
Monument, CO 80132-0767

To Diane Elise Jones,
for her sharp eyes and her uncanny instincts
as a reader

She sifts through our rough manuscripts
in order to rescue readers from
glitches that might otherwise have slipped through.

— 1 —

The enclosed areas of a Drifter colony never had any real weather, but today the skies of New Marrakech seemed gloomy and ominous. Like the day the Earth had been destroyed, ten years ago.

As she ran, Akima's silky, waist-length hair flew out behind her like a black banner rippling in a nonexistent breeze. She threaded her way through the tangled marketplace, called the souks, dodged past shops and down alleyways, taking shortcuts wherever she could find them. Without slowing, breath burning in her lungs, Akima ducked under awnings, jumped over a woven basket of exotic spice, and jostled other refugees from Earth who were as used to the crowds as she was.

Akima already knew most of the shortcuts. She and her grandmother had only moved here from Houston colony three years earlier to live with her uncle Yoshi, and she knew the intricate pathways through every neighborhood and shopping district as if she had been raised on New Marrakech since its beginning.

She had just received an emergency message about her grandmother. Tears stung her almond eyes, and she hoped she wasn't too late.

New Marrakech, like most Drifter colonies, had been formed by the fortunate Humans who escaped before the bloodthirsty Drej Mothership had blown up Earth. The energy-based aliens gave no reason for attacking humanity, and very little warning. And, after blasting the planet to rubble, the Drej had disappeared again, going dormant to recuperate after such an exhausting expenditure of energy.

Of the billions of Human beings on Earth, only a fraction had managed to get away in mismatched spaceships and long-distance transports. Without a homeworld, the Human refugees had clustered together in various systems throughout the Spiral Arm of the galaxy, linking their ships into hodgepodge colonies that drifted between planets. Sometimes the "Drifters" used an asteroid or barren moon as a base on which to build.

Muttering clipped apologies, Akima dodged a pair of freighter pilots who were buying kebabs from a street vendor; they raised their smoking skewers of meat and made wolf-whistles at her as she skirted the housewares bazaar. Ignoring the men, she ducked into a narrow passageway between a spice shop and a lamp gallery and emerged onto a street that was less crowded.

She whispered a prayer for her grandmother, hoping, *hoping*. At any other time Akima might have enjoyed the challenge in finding a route home that was faster than any she had used before, but today she found herself wondering impatiently why New Marrakech had to be one of the most complex and confusing of all Drifter colonies. The Earth ships clustered here had docked and anchored and linked with no plan whatsoever.

The colonists who could remember life on Earth taught the younger ones. For Akima, each of these stories, once learned, became a treasured possession. She had few actual memories of her childhood home or her parents. Her family had been split apart during the evacuation of Earth; some had never made it off the planet. But Akima's determined grandmother, Miwa Kunimoto, had found a transport vessel at the last minute and carried Akima onto it.

I don't know what I would have done without you, Grandmother, Akima thought. The words brought a lump to her throat again.

During the six years they had lived on Houston colony, Akima's grandmother had never stopped searching for her missing sisters, children, and grandchildren. A few years ago, she had located her son Yoshi, Akima's uncle, and had moved to New Marrakech to be close to him. Those had been happy times for Akima, living with a real family again. But last year, Uncle Yoshi had died of *pukra* fever, and now Akima's grandmother was ill.

On her desperate race home, Akima ducked beneath the awning of a sandal maker's shop, where a barely functional atmosphere filter coughed more dust than air, and dashed into an alley beside it. She clambered up the side of a building that had once been a cargo shuttle, flipped herself over the top of it, and dropped into the next alley over, saving herself several minutes. There was not a moment to lose.

Akima had grown up quickly. All children on Drifter colonies did. Every capable person was expected to work and contribute to the colony's survival. Children under the age of fourteen were allowed up to three hours a day for formal schooling, but the remainder of their learning came through apprenticeship and hard work.

Akima missed her classes now that she was too old to attend formal schooling, but her grandmother had supplemented her education. Each night her grandmother would sit for hours brushing Akima's long, glossy hair and telling her stories of Earth, of humanity's achievements, of heroes and villains. The stories comforted Akima, allowed her to hold on to her childhood for just a bit longer.

Akima worked inside a small short-range transport pod that had been converted into a communal bakery. One of the two engine cores had been adapted for use as an oven chamber, and the metal-walled vessel had become a place for families to bake their daily loaves and meet for fellowship with other Drifters. Akima didn't have any particular knack for making bread, but the baker had been a friend of her grandmother's, and he'd needed help.

Today, Akima felt defenseless and afraid.

Her grandmother, a martial arts instructor during more peaceful days on Earth, had spent part of every morning teaching her granddaughter the fundamentals of self-defense in over a dozen forms of martial arts. The training had left Akima with excellent reflexes, a limber body, and a superb sense of balance. Instruction in philosophy and meditation balanced her inside, as well, and gave her an air of confidence.

Despite Akima's self-assurance, however, she could not defend against death. Wiping flour from her cheek, she ducked through the door curtain and came to a panting halt inside their cozy little home. When she ran to her grandmother's bedside, Akima felt as if someone had activated a cryofield inside her stomach. She could sense what was happening, what was coming. Yet she refused to accept it.

The wise old woman was propped up on her cot. Akima knew she must be in pain, but her grandmother's face did not show it. "How did you get here so quickly, child?" The voice was weak, thin as rice paper.

She knelt, took her grandmother's hand, and said, "I'm sorry I kept you waiting. Maybe I shouldn't have gone to the bakery today."

Her grandmother smiled, and Akima could see that it took some effort to do so. "No regrets. You're here now, and I wanted to share this moment with you."

Akima's heart gave a lurch. "You'll feel better soon. Why don't you rest?"

Her grandmother shook her head, and even that small movement drained precious energy from her. "Now is all we have."

"Don't say that. You're going to be just fine." Tears welled up in Akima's eyes. She felt a touch, light as a warm breeze, on her hair. Her grandmother's hand.

"No tears for me, child. I have taught you since you were a young girl. You must know by now that I have no regrets. No unfinished business."

"But I still need you," Akima choked, finally looking at the old woman, hot droplets spilling down her cheeks.

Her grandmother touched one damp tear track. "Then if you must cry, be sad only for yourself."

"It's not fair," Akima whispered past the tightness in her throat. She was surprised to hear a tiny wheezing laugh in response.

"It is not *un*fair, child. No power in the universe can

guarantee that we ever have more than *now*—much less happiness or a long life. Many Humans forgot that . . . before the Drej came. But you have not forgotten, have you? I've taught you this lesson since we left Earth. Tell me what you've learned about the Now."

Akima didn't really want to recite what she had learned. It seemed such a waste of this precious time. But there was an urgency in her grandmother's voice that forced her to dredge her memory for the correct response. "The path to inner peace is not in the future. It is Now. Every moment offers its own choice of how it may be used," Akima summarized. "Only by choosing *now* to do what is good, what is right, what is best, can we acccpt our lives at every moment without regret."

"Yes, you know it," her grandmother said. "Never wait until tomorrow to do what is right."

Akima tried to keep her voice even. "But I don't know if I'm strong enough to use all the lessons you taught me."

The old woman sighed. "Then my only regret is that I will not be here to guide you. The healers say they can do nothing for me, and so I have chosen a teacher to help you, at least for a time."

A man cleared his throat in the dimness behind her, and Akima became aware for the first time that she was not alone with her grandmother. She had been so absorbed in the moment, she had never even noticed the tall, Islamic man seated quietly in the corner by the door. She recognized Mohammed Bourain, who worked as an instructor and master to apprentices in many fields on New Marrakech.

"You are stronger than you know, child," Akima's grandmother said in a voice so faint it was barely audible. "But Mohammed will teach you until you can stand on your own."

Akima looked into the old woman's face, ready to accept that their time together was nearing an end. Pushing away thoughts of sadness for a moment, she tried to think what was important *now*. What was the best use of the few moments they had left together?

"I love you," she said, her voice surprisingly strong. "You were a good teacher, and I'll remember everything I learned from you." Akima pressed her grandmother's withered hand to her damp cheek. "I promise you I'll always keep learning, and I won't put off doing what is right. I'll share your stories about Earth with other people. Thank you for sharing them with me, and for always being here for me."

She smiled a painful smile as a bittersweet realization swept over her. "You will always be there for me, Grandmother. I understand that now."

A glow seemed to light the old woman's face. The barest smile formed at the corners of her mouth, and she let out a contented sigh. She did not draw another breath.

Knowing that her sadness was for her own loss, Akima laid her head down beside her grandmother and wept.

— 2 —

While she remained alone in her private room, waiting for the time of the funeral, Akima took slow,
deep breaths. She gritted her teeth, clenched and unclenched her fists, staring at the sharp-edged, Japanese
ceremonial sword in front of her. She couldn't lose her
courage now.

In the lonely night after her grandmother had passed
away, Akima had already made the difficult decision—
now, the rest was just ritual. Her throat constricted, and
her eyes brimmed with moisture, which she quickly
brushed away.

"Grandmother is dead," she reminded herself, looking
down at the long, curved *wakazashi* blade. "What I do,
I do in her memory." But in the back of her mind, she
knew the old woman would not approve of what Akima
intended to do.

A heavy emptiness weighed at the bottom of her
stomach like a leaden whirlpool that drained away her

sorrow and her fear, leaving only stern determination in its wake. Akima drew another deep, deliberate breath, letting her mind fill with peaceful resolve.

In her chamber, she scanned all the trinkets and Earth mementos her grandmother had given her over the years: an old alarm clock, a horse statuette, a snow globe, a stuffed bunny, a baseball, a teacup. A faint smile curved the corners of her full mouth as Akima let each treasure bring back memories of time spent with her grandmother and stories she had told.

"Lights on full," she said. Then, turning her back to the mementos, she faced the mirror. In her reflection, Akima's hair glowed a rich black—the hair her grandmother had always brushed for her. She picked up the sharp ceremonial blade. No one would be here to assist her. Akima had asked for this time alone during the funeral preparations, and her friends had seemed to understand. Now there was nothing left to do but prepare for the ritual.

Breathe in, breathe out. Slow, relaxed. Holding the *wakazashi* in her right hand, she gathered her long, thick hair in her left hand and held it well away from her neck.

She brought the sword slashing down.

Drifter funerals were sober rituals, developed by people who had been forced to leave their planet behind, who had already lost so much. On New Marrakech, the ceremonies were kept as short as possible, attended only by close friends and family members—if the colonist had been lucky enough to have any surviving family.

Her grandmother's body had been placed floating at the center of a small no-grav dome, and Akima, her hair newly cropped short, hovered beside Mohammed

Bourain. The thirty or so mourners arranged themselves in a circle around the old woman, set the circle turning, then orbited the body, like a string of planets around a burned-out star. Akima couldn't speak first, but each mourner shared a sentence or two of memories, taking turns, never pausing either in their words or their movements until the end.

Words of appreciation rippled around the circle, approaching Akima.

"She helped me find my son, who was on New Bangkok."

"She taught me how to defend myself."

"She tended me for two days when I was sick."

"I was always at peace in her presence."

At last, Mohammed spoke, "She was a fellow teacher, lit from within by the flame of hope. Even after her death, that flame still burns."

Finally, the circle had gone all the way around and reached her. Akima's voice was strong and steady as she spoke. "My grandmother loved people, and she loved Earth, and she loved me. Every day she shared her memories with me. I will share those stories, as well, with anyone who will listen. Her flame of hope has not died, and her memories will live on." Akima paused, then began the final words of the funeral ceremony. "She was born on Earth."

"She was born on Earth," the mourners in the circle intoned.

"Earth is gone, but its memory remains."

The circle again echoed her words.

"Our friend is gone, but her memory remains."

As they repeated the hushed litany, the drifting circle grabbed handholds and everyone faced the center.

"This was a thing she loved in her life," Akima said, pushing forward to reach her grandmother's body, drifting weightless. From a pocket in her mourning robe she withdrew a braided length of her silky black hair. Akima placed it on her grandmother's chest and folded the fragile, lifeless hands around it.

"Goodbye, Grandmother," she whispered. "I'll remember everything you taught me."

After the funeral, Akima could not remember accompanying Mohammed back to his house at the edge of the souks. Had they walked? Had they taken hoverscooters? She'd been so absorbed in her thoughts that she had no recollection.

From the outside, Mohammed's home was nothing to look at, one doorway among many on a crowded street of dwellings. It must once have been a cargo container from a long-range ore hauler, refitted as a separate structure to create a house. But the moment she stepped through the entrance, Akima was transported to a place of enchantment. A waist-high tiled fountain trickled at the center of a miniature square courtyard; the walls were ornamented with plaz-tile mosaic work. A keyhole-shaped doorway led from the tiny courtyard through a purple curtain to an inner chamber.

At the curtained doorway, they removed their shoes and stepped inside onto plush rugs woven with geometric designs. Billowing cloth hung from the ceiling and down the walls, giving the impression of being inside a silken tent. Hassocks and cushions were strewn on the floor around a low table. Half-hidden lights twinkled from the ceiling.

Onc of the doors opened and a young boy, at least

two years her junior, entered the room. He was half a head shorter than she was, with dark curly hair, olive skin, and striking green eyes.

"This is my son, Ishaq," Mohammed said. He glanced at the boy. "As I told you, Akima is coming to live with us."

Ishaq offered her a shy smile. "You're welcome here, Akima. As you can see, we have plenty of room."

Mohammed gave her a small, formal bow. "We will be your family now."

"How many . . . ?" Akima's voice trailed off.

"Just the two of us," Mohammed said.

"My father's a really good cook," Ishaq said. "Are you hungry? We have prepared a complete family-style meal to welcome you."

To her great surprise after the sadness of the day, Akima found that she was starving. A full, multicourse Moroccan meal was normally reserved for very special occasions.

Mohammed rubbed his hands together. "Good. Is everything ready, Ishaq?"

Ishaq nodded. "You left very complete instructions."

"Then let's begin. Please be seated. I will serve you myself."

Ishaq and Akima made themselves comfortable on cushions beside the low table while Mohammed ducked into the next room. He returned with an engraved silver basin and a steaming pitcher of water, and she and Ishaq held their hands out over the basin. Mohammed poured the warm, cleansing water first over their hands, then over his own.

Next, Mohammed brought them each a small bowl of soup made from lentils grown in the Drifters' hydro-

ponic gardens, along with freshly baked bread. Though
Akima had lived on this colony for three years, she'd
rarely tasted food this good. Next came a platter of as-
sorted cold salads, all of which they ate with their hands:
preserved olives, pickled potatoes, diced vegetables with
savory spices, and cubes of fruit sprinkled with flower-
scented water.

The next course consisted of a pastry made from flaky
dough filled with eggs, spices, chopped nuts, and ground
tingabird meat dusted with fine sugar. The meat course
was a glotfowl, roasted with olives and lemons in a
small clay pot. They ended their meal with syrup-soaked
finger pastries and tea made from dried mint leaves.

With each new course, Mohammed told a story about
the Earth dish that it was based on and what the original
ingredients had been in ancient times. Whenever he left
the room, Ishaq took the opportunity to tell Akima more
about his father; the boy loved to talk. Mohammed had
been involved in a division of the famous Titan Project,
though not the most controversial part, directed by the
scientist Sam Tucker.

"Did you notice all the artistic and cultural touches in
our home?" Ishaq asked, indicating an especially exqui-
site Buddha figurine. "Those were a part of my father's
work. He thinks it's very important to preserve our heritage. As a matter of fact, he says it's as much a part of
humanity's hope for the future as any other part of the
Titan Project." He shrugged. "That's why my father became a teacher when we got to New Marrakech. He told
me he taught your grandmother the mythology of
Earth's southern hemisphere."

Akima nodded, her heart still heavy each time she

thought of her lost grandmother. "Does he teach anything else?"

Ishaq laughed. "Almost everything: reading, arithmetic, Earth languages, cooking, art—any part of Human culture. My father says that if we keep our culture alive, humanity will survive. Someday, someone will lead us to a new place, a new homeworld we'll be able to call our own."

They were lofty, idealistic-sounding words, but Akima knew better than to express skepticism. Ishaq and Mohammed were very serious in their hope for the future. Perhaps someday mankind *would* find a new home.

After all, Akima just had.

— 3 —

A year later, Akima thought she might find content-
ment again. Her life had settled down, and she had
actually begun to think about being happy.

Then the Drej arrived and changed all that. . . .

Akima lived with Mohammed and his son as part of their
family, fiercely independent and eager to learn what she
could. Mohammed was a hard taskmaster, utterly fo-
cused on the things that interested him. He was incred-
ibly intelligent and full of stories about the achievements
of mankind, the great painters and musicians and artists.
He was particularly fond of Mozart.

He showed her and Ishaq images of sculptures and
architecture—the Parthenon, the Eiffel Tower, the Pyr-
amids of Egypt, the Great Hassan II Mosque in
Casablanca, the extravagant casinos of Las Vegas. He
loved his small Buddha statuette, proudly displayed on
a shelf in their main living area. Each example had a

particularly Human stamp that seemed more magnificent than the wonders of the Spiral Arm so often touted by alien traders passing through the Drifter colony.

Though she and her grandmother had moved from Houston colony—where she had fond memories of her childhood—Akima had never once considered returning there. On New Marrakech the Drifters formed a tightly woven society where everyone helped everyone else, where loyalty and friendship counted for more than individual wealth or success. She devoted herself to helping Mohammed in all facets of his work.

Akima still spent many pleasant hours looking at the trinkets her grandmother had left her, keepsakes taken from old Earth during their scrambled evacuation. She had been too young to understand much about Earth when the aliens broke through its outer defenses and charged in to destroy the home planet of humanity, but she held on to these reminders.

While Ishaq and the formal pupils studied under his father's tutelage, Akima often spent her days out in the streets of New Marrakech doing errands for Mohammed. Occasionally, she still helped out at the bakery, but she preferred to be out in the souks, memorizing the labyrinth of the bazaar in greater detail than any map could ever show. The stalls and awnings changed weekly, and no one could keep track of it all. Except Akima.

Mohammed had sent her out this afternoon to meet a Human captain due to arrive at New Marrakech. It hadn't taken him long to realize that she could do errands more efficiently than any paid runners, and Akima enjoyed the freedom to wander through the colony.

"Captain Korso was a friend of Sam Tucker's," Mohammed had told her. "He's the only man known to have seen Tucker after he escaped in the *Titan* ship during the Drej attack on Earth." Mohammed's dark eyes grew misty, and Akima could tell he was replaying the destruction in his mind. Most living Humans had watched that horror, and it had haunted their nightmares ever since. "Korso says he has Sam Tucker's last log."

Mohammed had drawn a long breath. "Ah, how I would love to hear the man speak again." Then he snapped back to reality and lit two more candles to increase the light inside their small home. "Go meet him when the *Valkyrie* docks, Akima. Pick up the datacard or—if you can—bring Captain Korso back here, while I finish my classes for the day."

"Nothing I can't handle," Akima had assured him. Touched by Mohammed's sense of wonder, she had raced through the streets to the outer docking ports. Since most other alien races shunned the Drifters, space traffic consisted primarily of Human refugees, traders, and businessmen who preferred to make their way across the galactic trade routes rather than longing for a new homeworld. These merchants brought vital supplies, since the Drifters were not self-sufficient: They needed to import water, food, building materials, even air.

Now, Akima stood under the docking hub beneath the crackling atmosphere field. She watched a variety of vessels attach themselves to the docks, connected to a central hub by atmosphere tunnels. Pilots and passengers entered the enclosed Drifter colony, filing papers and checking databases for family members lost during the frantic evacuation of Earth. Some ships had been linked to the docking bays here for so long that they might as well be permanent fixtures on New Marrakech.

A decade ago, the ships that escaped Earth had gathered with common interests, nationalities, or religious creeds, like independent countries scattered across the Spiral Arm. Due to the Drej threat, scattering the race like grains of rice increased their safety. No single alien attack could wipe them all out again. But it made Akima sad to know that humanity no longer had a heart, a central home. . . .

A family of Australian survivors loaded supplies into a radiation-scarred passenger pod (barely capable of moving under its own power), ready to brave the wilds of space to start their own new colony. Akima watched the wide-eyed children and the eager, ambitious parents. She hoped they would survive the journey to wherever they were going. If the Australians did find an unclaimed habitable world, they would have enough difficulties just setting up their homestead. . . .

Merchants, antique sellers, and curiosity seekers pressed forward as each large ship docked. They were anxious to discover what the vessels carried, what unusual artifacts or food supplies or strange wares the owners might have for sale.

Through the broad kleersteel windows, she observed the moving dots of light, spacecraft cruising toward the Drifter colony or on their way to nearby Solbrecht. Captain Korso's ship, the *Valkyrie*, had already filed an approach plan. While most Human refugees preferred to huddle together in Drifter colonies, a few enterprising souls found work among the alien races, or worked for themselves. Like Korso.

She watched the *Valkyrie* approach, impressed by its sleek lines. The ship was a long, fast vessel with an elliptical bridge section and an extended waspish body, complete with swept-back guidance fins, good for atmospheric flight or for tearing across open space. Looking like an armored falcon, the *Valkyrie* approached its designated docking port, and Akima noticed that the pilot seemed uncomfortable handling the big craft. Tractor beams and laser docking guides helped the ship link up, but for all its fast lines and trim contours, the *Valkyrie* seemed underutilized.

Maybe this captain needed a pilot. . . . Akima longed to fly her own vessel someday, to travel the Spiral Arm and see what the universe had to offer, face all the challenges the galaxy might hold. But until she had some training, she had no chance of getting any such job.

When the airlock hissed open, a tall, handsome Human swaggered out into the atmosphere tunnel. He had a short goatee, brown hair, and an abundance of confidence. His blue eyes were bright, flashing around as he studied his surroundings.

Akima came forward, and he spotted her immediately. "Captain Korso? I was sent here to meet you."

The man looked her over and produced a strange smile somewhere between suspicion and amusement. "Where's Mohammed?"

"I'm his student. He sent me for the datacard, or I'd be happy to lead you to our home. Mohammed was hoping you could stay for dinner, or at least tea."

A troubled expression crossed Korso's face. "Afraid I can't, kid. I'm on a tight schedule. A few deliveries of perishables to go straight to Solbrecht, and then I'm off to Krondor." His smile softened, as if he were sharing a secret. "It's spore season, you know, and they only fly for two weeks. If I get there fast enough, I'll snag a cargo load that'll sell for a big profit."

At the captain's mention of profit, Akima realized that

Mohammed had given her no money, nothing to trade for the datacard she was supposed to retrieve. She had hoped they would pay Korso at home after a long dinner and conversation, perhaps after a bit of haggling.

"You'll have to come with me back to Mohammed if you need payment for this," Akima said.

Korso frowned, wrestling with his thoughts. He looked at his chronometer, then back at the *Valkyrie* at the other end of the docking tube. Akima noticed that the engines remained warm and prepped. This captain was really anxious to depart.

"I really don't have time, kid." Korso reached into his pocket and withdrew a datacard. "Consider it a gift for Mohammed. I knew Sam Tucker, too, and he'd want this passed on to anyone who worked on the Titan Project."

Akima said, "I've heard so many stories about Sam Tucker—"

"Yeah, I was there when he took off from Earth. I watched the *Titan* lift off just as those Drej clowns broke through the defense grid. I'll never forget the sight." Korso's face went slack, and he shuddered. He feigned a smile for her. "I just don't like the Drej, kid. Don't even like to think about them."

She accepted the datacard and turned it over in her hands. It looked so small, so insignificant—yet its information might be important to Mohammed in his work. "Thank you, Captain Korso. I hope I see you again."

Korso raised his eyebrows. "The universe is a big place . . . but there's always a chance." Without even setting foot on New Marrakech, Korso turned back to the *Valkyrie*. "Tell Mohammed that I . . ." He paused and swallowed hard. "That I wish him good luck." Then he briskly climbed back up the connecting tube into his ship. The docking hatch glided shut.

Puzzled by Korso's rush, Akima stayed at the docking area and watched other ships attach themselves to New Marrakech. Korso was so anxious to take off that he barely waited for full clearance. The *Valkyrie* streaked away, nearly ramming a blocky cargo ship that chugged toward the Drifter colony.

Tapping a finger thoughtfully against her full lips, Akima shook her head. Akima was an impatient person herself, but one of the things she'd learned from Mohammed—and from her grandmother before that—was to savor all the time she had, to develop a sense of inner peace. Captain Korso, on the other hand, seemed a total stranger to patience and calm.

Akima lost track of time as the vessels came and went in a hypnotic pattern. She never grew tired of the variety of spacecraft designs, powerful or weak engines, nuclear propulsion or combustion rocket motors.

But after a while, the knot of approaching spacecraft suddenly swirled about, each one taking evasive action like a herd of goats disturbed by a hungry wolf. An alarm rang through New Marrakech—an ominous tone she had never heard before. Akima looked around her as the crowd began to panic.

In the star-strewn sky overhead, glowing blue forms streaked close, nineteen sharp-edged, angular warships. Though it had been many years, Akima recognized the attack craft instantly. Drej Stingers!

In tight formation, the alien vessels arrowed in toward the unarmed colony and spread out, preparing for their destructive run. The citizens of New Marrakech broke and ran screaming for shelter before the first blast even hit.

Akima stood frozen in awe, remembering what she had seen as a girl, ships taking off from Earth in all directions, her grandmother gripping her wrist so tightly that she had wailed from the pain, but the old woman refused to let go. Akima yelled for her mother, her father, even for her big brother, but they had all become separated in the rush toward available ships. Her grandmother had carried her aboard the nearest craft, firmly moving people out of the way. Other refugees clawed at Akima, grabbed her clothes, tried to snatch the tiny satchel of personal possessions clutched in her hand.

The evacuation ship had been like a cattle car, terrified people pressed face-to-face, shoulder-to-shoulder, and when not one more person could get on board, the doors were sealed shut. Fingers clawed for the opening and armed guards shot at crowds to keep them back.

Overhead in the blue sky, Drej Stingers had appeared. Back then, little Akima had seen only a glimpse before the evacuation ship became dark—before her world was filled with a rumbling roar as the engines blasted, tearing them away from Earth's gravity. Except for her uncle, she had never seen the rest of her family again. . . .

Now, on New Marrakech, the Stingers had appeared once more, like a recurring nightmare. As the first explosions ripped through the sealed hulls of the outer storage pods and disrupted the atmosphere containment fields, Akima thrust the valuable datacard into her pocket, then raced along the crowded streets.

The Drej ships flew overhead, attacking at will. Rubble fell and hungry flames licked upward. Already the ground was strewn with bodies, some moaning, some quiet.

Blood trickled into Akima's eye. A piece of shrapnel had cut her forehead near the hairline, and she hadn't even felt it. Collapsing buildings toppled to the streets and rampant fires spread. The Drej bombardment continued.

Akima ran at full speed. She had to get back to Mohammed and Ishaq. She could think of nothing else.

— 4 —

U nder attack, the already-confusing souks became total chaos.

People ran screaming in all directions, and Akima had
to fight her way forward, trying to get home. She ducked
jabbing elbows, tripped over flowing robes, pushed
deeper into New Marrakech while the rest of the population fled outward to the space docks, hoping to climb
aboard a retreating vessel.

Echoes from booming explosions rippled down the
tangled streets. Akima's ears popped from a sudden
pressure drop, and she knew with a sick feeling that one
of the atmosphere containment fields had failed catastrophically; bulkhead doors slammed down to prevent
further air loss, trapping some victims on the wrong side.
Overhead, lightning crackled as a blast struck the force-
field sky, and shimmering ions sparkled like fireworks.

Akima ran through the frantic crowds. In the complex
souks, food vendors' stalls had caught on fire as cooking

braziers and heating plates were overturned. Greasy smoke swirled through the air, and striped awnings burst into orange flame. Fleeing families broke through stall barricades, pushing tables and benches aside to make new walkways where no paths had been before. Baskets of sage, oregano, and cayenne pepper were trampled underfoot, sending clouds of pungent seasonings into the air.

Akima saw heavy canvas folds tumbling like parachutes onto piles of merchandise. A sharp, curved blade poked through the fabric and then sawed downward. A knife maker's stall had collapsed on top of the man, and he was using one of his own daggers to slash himself free.

Bending over, sneezing from the dusty spices in the air, Akima grabbed the edge of the cut and helped tear the fabric until the bearded man pushed his arms and shoulders through. Tears ran down his face, and he scrambled out, breathing hard. Ornate, curved blades that had fallen from display racks clattered all around him. He brushed himself off and heaved great gulps of the spice-congested air. "Thank you! Thank you, my child!" His reddened, puffy eyes looked at her with an embarrassing amount of gratitude. "Here, take this dagger as a token of my thanks. Here, choose another."

"Sorry, I don't have time," she said, but accepted the knife. "Thank you. I'll give it back if we all get out of this."

"No need. My gift to you with my thanks. Wait. Here, let me give—"

But Akima ran off, tucking the dagger into her sash. She finally approached a section of the Drifter colony that looked familiar, despite the smoke and destruction. Nearly home.

In the darkening sky above, she watched an old ship loaded with refugees blast free from the docking rings. They escaped into space—until two Stingers opened fire on it, vaporizing the vessel and all the helpless people aboard. Inside the colony, flaming rubble crashed like meteors onto the haphazard dwellings.

"Ishaq!" she shouted. "Mohammed!" She raced down her street, ducking under torn awnings. The thick smoke made her cough.

From the other end of a crooked alley, she heard the voice of a boy yelling. "Akima! There you are. We were so worried." Ishaq raced toward her.

"Where's your father?" Akima said.

"I'm not sure," Ishaq said. "He left the house with me, but when we started looking for you, I lost him." The two of them searched about, shouting Mohammed's name at the top of their lungs.

Uncontrolled fires spread down the enclosed streets, out of sight behind tall buildings. An explosion ripped open the sky, and a detonating warehouse sprayed a geyser of water from a storage tank. People fled toward the tall, silvery minaret of the rocketship that had been converted into the central mosque of New Marrakech.

"Mohammed!" Akima yelled again.

Wide-eyed and gasping, the tall man finally emerged from a side street. His dark hair was bedraggled, his face drawn with concern, but when he saw Akima and Ishaq, his shoulders slumped with relief. "There you are, children! I was so worried I wouldn't find you again in this madness."

"We're safe," Akima said. "For now."

"We have to get off New Marrakech somehow." Mohammed suddenly looked at her. "Did you meet Korso? Did you get the datacard?"

Akima withdrew the card from her pocket. "Here, the last logs of Sam Tucker."

Tears welled in Mohammed's eyes. "So close! This might hold news that could make a difference for us. But keep it safe for now."

Ishaq looked down the street, blinking furiously. "We could go to the docking ports. That's where everybody else is headed."

"There aren't enough ships for all of us," Mohammed said.

The ground lurched beneath their feet, and Akima knew the Drifter colony had been knocked off its axis. Soon, some of the main gravity generators would surely fail, as well as the vital atmosphere containment fields. All around them flames rose higher, consuming fabric and perishables in the ramshackle dwellings, racing toward their home.

A new wave of alarm crashed like a tsunami across Mohammed's face. "My material! I have to save the items entrusted to me." He raced toward their doorway. "You two stay here, but I must go back inside. These things are irreplaceable."

The tall man ducked into the tiny courtyard and through the curtained, keyhole doorway as a trio of Drej Stingers cruised overhead, blasting indiscriminately. The alien attackers fired energy bursts that ruptured metal-walled tanks and broke clustered buildings free and sent them tumbling into space. The Drej circled around and fired again, annihilating the helpless vessels.

One block over, a tall metal construction, the remnants of what had been a spacetug, groaned and snapped its support struts. Broken electrical cables sparked and sizzled as the abandoned ship tipped and slid. Akima looked up and saw the mountain of metal toppling toward their house.

"Mohammed!" she cried.

Ishaq took three sprinting steps toward the courtyard entrance before Akima caught him by the collar and knocked him aside. Together, they rolled to the left just as debris crashed down in the street. The spacetug flattened several low dwellings and rolled over to crash through the roof of Mohammed's home.

"No!" Ishaq screamed, clawing free of Akima's grasp.

Flames caught on the rooftops, and the ruined spacetug slid to one side, crashing into the opposite block.

The remnants of their home lay smashed and burning. "Come on, Ishaq!" Akima cried. "We have to get him out of there."

The fountain in the tiny courtyard had been broken and overturned. Frantically she ripped up portions of the toppled wall plates, lifting hollow structural beams. Ishaq assisted her, his face streaked with soot and grime.

"Mohammed, are you there?" she called. "Mohammed, say something so we can find you."

"Father! Answer us!"

Encroaching flames licked at the walls, catching the broken material on fire. Overhead, a stretched barrier of canvas snapped as the blaze ate through the fibers and consumed the frame.

Akima and Ishaq shoved wreckage aside: cooking pots, stubby candles, tangled clothes that had tumbled from storage cubicles. A fresh pot of tea had fallen over, spilling minty-scented liquid onto the patterned rugs.

Then Akima saw Mohammed's hand protruding from under a collapsed portion of the wall. "He's here, Ishaq. Help me!"

Together, the two of them knocked over furniture, pulling away hastily packed boxes of Earth keepsakes that until now they had displayed so proudly on their shelves. Akima remembered Mohammed telling her about each one, why the objects were so special. Then, to her vast relief, she heard the tall man groan. "He's still alive!" she said.

When they managed to remove most of the debris, Akima saw that Mohammed had been injured in many places. Bright blood stained his colorful jalaba. His arm hung limp at an awkward angle, and his face was bruised. But she feared that he had far worse internal injuries. And she knew with an even greater sense of dread that she would find no hospital, no medical assistance in the midst of this attack.

"We've got to help him ourselves," she said.

Flames rose higher at the sides of the dwelling. The smoke inside made the air so thick they could barely see, barely breathe. "We can't leave him here," Ishaq said. "What are we going to do?"

"We're going to do our best," Akima said, grabbing a purple robe from a pile nearby and wrapping it around her nose and mouth to filter some of the smoke from the air. She handed a jalaba to Ishaq, who followed her lead.

One of Mohammed's hands clutched the beautiful Buddha figurine he had always treasured. In his other hand, he held a holoscroll, a data container that he had considered important enough to risk dying for. But he wasn't dead yet.

"We shouldn't move him," Ishaq said, his face above

the filtering cloth pasty with sweat from fear and deep concern for his father.

Akima jerked her head to indicate the rising flames. "We don't have any choice."

Together, they carried the tall man out of the rubble and into the open street. Mohammed gasped and groaned. He continued to bleed profusely.

"Ishaq, give me that jalaba. We can tear it up to make bandages." Akima unwound the cloth from her nose and mouth, and Ishaq did the same. He began tearing the cloth into strips while Akima sat beside Mohammed, applying pressure to a heavily bleeding wound, feeling helpless and at a loss.

As the Drej continued to attack and New Marrakech went up in flames around them, she wondered if any of them would survive the next few hours.

— 5 —

Mohammed lay severely injured under questionable shelter in the street. Akima was so determined to find help for him that she barely noticed the pandemonium around them.

"Why do the sirens keep wailing?" Ishaq moaned, covering his ears, flushed and terrified. "Everyone on the whole colony knows about the emergency by now!" He looked helplessly down at his father, bleeding and unconscious. Ishaq had run out of cloth to tear up and didn't know what else to do.

Secondary explosions rippled through the hodgepodge of vessels and structures, but miraculously the main atmosphere fields continued to hold. Doomed refugees remained trapped inside several isolated containers as atmosphere and debris bled through hull breaches and out into space.

"I know something that might help him!" Desperate,

Ishaq ducked back into their wrecked dwelling before Akima could yell for him to be careful.

Lying in front of her, Mohammed stirred, then coughed blood. She gingerly touched his side, found darkening bruises under the skin, an angry purplish color that implied internal bleeding. She had stanched the flow of blood from a wound in his shoulder, but his ribs moved in unexpected ways, broken ends clicking together. Mohammed's dark eyes were glazed and narrow, as if he saw something deep within his mind, but couldn't express his thoughts. He spoke unintelligible words in Arabic, and Akima wished his son was there to hear him. Ishaq would have understood.

The man's hands clutched and grasped, searching for something. Akima held out the alabaster Buddha figurine and the holoscroll that he had tried to rescue from the house. "I've got them, Mohammed—whatever they are," she said.

He seemed to hear her and relaxed slightly, his shoulders slumping against the street. "Tell Ishaq . . . location . . . treasures. Hope of Earth." She brushed a hand over his sweaty forehead, trying to soothe him.

Smudged with grime, Ishaq raced back into the street from the burning dwelling, his arms laden with a clutter of books and datapads. He could barely carry them all, and one volume slipped from his grasp and dropped onto the street. The boy scuttled forward, knelt, and dumped his load of books beside his father. Behind him, their home continued to burn.

"These are all the medical texts I could find," he said. "There's a first aid manual here somewhere." Ishaq flipped through the datapads and books, discarding one after another until finally he hefted a volume on the diagnosis and treatment of injuries.

Akima watched the young man search with mounting frustration for answers in the printed volumes. He didn't seem to understand the technical terms. "Subdural hema . . . This is no help." He picked up a first aid datapad. "Bandages—check. Analgesics—not really. Blanket, water. . . ."

"Got it," Akima said. She raced down the street to a small fountain that was used for ceremonial washing and ablutions before prayers. After soaking rags, she came back to wipe the blood from Mohammed's face and clean some of his injuries. Ishaq had tucked his father's robe around him as a makeshift blanket, but Akima knew that would not help him enough. "We have to get him some medical attention. A real doctor."

Ishaq continued to scroll through the first aid datapad, intently comparing diagrams and descriptions, then shook his head and scrolled to another section. He looked up at her, his face plaintive and lost. "But *where,* Akima? The Drifter hospitals have been bombed like everything else. There are thousands of injured people. We'll never get help for him in time."

Overhead, through the sparkling remnants of the atmosphere field well away from the Drej Stingers, she saw a large ship approaching, a medical emergency vessel from nearby Solbrecht. Responding to the Drej attack, some medical specialists had launched their vessel in hopes of charging for rescue services; they would never have risked the ire of the Drej simply for humanitarian reasons.

When she saw the hospital ship cruising above the colony, Akima knew that was their only chance. "I'm going to find a comm system," she said. "I'll summon some help." She left Ishaq with his injured father and his books.

"Just hurry," Ishaq said. "I'm not sure what else we can do for him."

Exhausted but intent on her mission, Akima raced through the once-familiar streets where her neighbors had become panicked strangers. The wreckage and smoke had made well-known areas into a confusion of dead ends and lost hopes. A merchandise bazaar that had once displayed preserved fruits and fresh, homegrown herbs had been abandoned, the stalls a scatter of upended baskets, toppled benches, and broken tables.

One thick-walled structure made from an armored cargo container was a moneylender's office and banking station. Akima went to the door, found it ajar, and slid the hatch aside. All the moneylender's currency vaults had automatically sealed during the attack, but the tables and cubicles remained in place. *Including the communications systems.*

Akima threw herself into a chair and switched on a broad-spectrum frequency, calling out to anyone who would listen. "I urgently request assistance for a severely injured man. Please respond! I need instructions and medical help."

The screen displayed only static, but she knew that someone on the Solbrecht medical station had to answer her. "Can anybody hear me? I've got an injured man—"

Finally an image formed, showing the gaunt, gray-skinned form of one of the Solbrecht natives. His large, amber eyes appeared frightened, flashing with reflected light. "You and everyone else." All four of his arms waved about from control panel to documentation pad, keeping busy. "There are too many injured parties from this attack. We cannot handle all of them."

"But he needs help." Akima wouldn't back down, thinking of all the rare items Mohammed had collected. "We can pay you."

"Very well, bring the victim up here to our facility, and we'll tend him like all the rest, provided you can afford our services." The alien turned his head and shouted instructions to a bustling paramedic crew rushing through corridors on the hospital ship.

Akima knew she would find a way to meet the price, if necessary. What she didn't have was a way off of New Marrakech—especially not in the midst of this frantic evacuation. Through the dampening atmosphere fields, she heard the whine and groan of more vessels lifting off, a final few ships breaking free and striking out into open space.

"We have no way to get off the colony," she transmitted again, but the frantic Solbrecht orderly turned away as more casualties were brought in. He offered a variety of confusing gestures with all four arms. Over the channel she heard moans from injured Humans aboard the medical ship. Solbrecht doctors called orders, shouting for Human medicharts. None of the aliens seemed to have any specialty in Human anatomy.

Then the image faded as the orderly cut her off, breaking the connection. Akima pounded on the controls and the inputpad, adjusting frequencies, boosting transmission power until she finally reestablished contact. The amber-eyed orderly looked as if he wanted to disconnect the communications system entirely. "I have work to do here. Your continued interruptions may endanger lives. We are already flooded with patients to tend to."

"I know," Akima replied, "and there are lots more down here on New Marrakech. You have to send help down to the colony—not just for my friend, but hundreds of others, maybe thousands. I don't know. The streets are in flames, buildings have collapsed. We urgently need medical help."

Multiarmed Solbrecht doctors rushed past the orderly. The alien turned around and finally, with a last glance at Akima, said, "Even if we had ambulance shuttles to spare, we could not come down to treat any victims. All of our facilities are *up here,* all of our medicine, and surgeons, and operating chambers. We can help your friend only if you are able to get him here, to the hospital ship."

Without waiting for her response, the orderly switched off, leaving Akima cold and alone inside the moneylender's chamber. She knew what she had to do. There was no other choice.

Somehow, Akima had to secure a functioning ship and get Mohammed on board with Ishaq tending him. She would sacrifice her own seat if necessary. Her mentor would never survive unless she could get him up to that orbiting hospital.

To her relief, she noticed that the Drej attack had waned. The alien ships drew back as if to view the smoldering ruins of New Marrakech. Apparently, they had done all the damage that interested them. She left the banking facility behind and bounded through smashed fruit and shattered jars that smelled of pungent vinegar and sweet syrup. The panic had begun to subside with the retreat of the Stingers, yet the wreckage of New Marrakech continued to burn. The colonists would need every able body to help put out fires and search for survivors, but Akima had to get away.

She passed an old man who sat on an ornate leather sling-chair. He lounged back, seemingly unaffected by the terror and evacuation. He had brought his seat out to where he could watch New Marrakech receive its pummeling. Clearly, he had made up his mind to die there, if that was his fate, but he refused to join the mobs rushing for a way out.

Akima stopped by him. "I need a ship. I have to get medical help."

The old man nodded toward the docking ring. "Not too many vessels left."

"I have to find one," she said. "My friend was trapped in the rubble. Now he's bleeding, and I need a doctor."

"What you need is far away," he said. "But if you hurry, you might stop one of those last vessels." He closed his eyes, drew a deep breath of smoky-smelling air. Akima saw that he had dismissed her, and so she raced on.

The flow of people had crowded toward the docking tube and an airlock of one of the last vessels that was still connected to the colony. She saw an old-model ship that aficionados would have called a "classic," but which most would see as a clunky workhorse that had outlived its time.

The ship's engines were firing, sputtering, trying to take hold. Drifters pushed toward the airlock tube, battering on the sealed door as if they meant to breach the containment and kill everyone. Akima looked up in despair, saw that she would never get aboard. She would never convince the pilot to wait for her to bring Mohammed and Ishaq.

Akima wanted to cry, but that would serve no purpose. She had cried enough in her life, and now she needed to solve problems.

As the ship tore free of its docking connectors, the crowded refugees of New Marrakech let out a collective, angry moan. Now Akima could see the side of the vessel, a hand-lettered name on its hull in clumsy writing, as if a child had painted them on: *Sword Ring*.

She wondered who the pilot and passengers were aboard that ship. She wished them well, even as other Drifters shook their fists and howled in outrage. They were all stuck here.

At least the Drej were leaving. The Drej Stingers circled the colony one last time and flew off, still in perfect formation, apparently not interested in obliterating the Human survivors, just in hurting them. And the Drej had hurt the Humans indeed. . . .

Like Mohammed . . .

But Akima knew how to be resourceful. There *had* to be another way. Fearing that she was too late, that she had wasted too much time here at the docking ring, she ran back toward Ishaq and Mohammed.

She simply had to find another alternative.

— 6 —

By the time Akima returned, sweating and out of breath with desperation, Ishaq had placed strategic bandages on Mohammed's wounds. The boy had recovered a few medical supplies from their crushed house, which was now reduced to smoldering piles of rubble.

Ishaq's expression was grave. "I've done all I can." He gestured helplessly to the open medical texts strewn on the street. "It could be too many things, too many injuries inside. I can't proceed without diagnostic instruments or real medicines."

Trying to catch her breath, Akima managed a grim nod. "I've talked to the hospital ship from Solbrecht. They'll treat Mohammed, but only if we can get him up there ourselves." She had run until her lungs burned from the acrid smoke curling up through the war zone. "We can't wait for someone to rescue us."

Ishaq looked suddenly hopeful again. "Have you found a ship? Did you go to the docking rings?"

She shook her head, unable to take her eyes from Mohammed's form. "No available spacecraft, only mobs trying to grab any ship that's ready to take off. Half of New Marrakech has evacuated already."

Ishaq's narrow shoulders slumped. "Then what can we do?"

Akima drew a deep breath and raised her chin. "We're going to find our own way." Her almond eyes flashed, hard and determined.

"But if all the pilots have taken their vessels—"

"Then we'll just have to get ourselves another ship and another pilot." She swallowed hard. "Even if it has to be me."

"You can't fly a ship," Ishaq said.

"There's always a first time," Akima said, pushing strands of hair out of her eyes. "I've watched them take off enough times, and you can help me out by reading the manuals."

"That's crazy!"

"Would you rather just give up and let your father die?" She crossed her arms over her chest.

Ishaq set his jaw. "No. Tell me what to do."

"First, we need a stretcher. It's the only way we can carry him." She did not voice the obvious, though—that she had no idea where they would take him.

Akima rushed into one of the smashed, abandoned homes on the street and came out with a battered light-weight cot, while Ishaq tore a sheet of red and green cloth from an awning into strips.

"Lift him gently," Ishaq warned. "He might have broken ribs. I read in one of the manuals that broken bones could puncture his lungs or his spleen."

"We shouldn't be moving him at all," Akima muttered, "but I can't think of any other way."

Mohammed groaned deep in his throat. He raised his head, blinking glazed eyes, then he slumped back, passing out again.

Akima sighed in relief, knowing that her mentor felt no pain now. Together they lifted Mohammed onto the cot. They used some cloth strips from the awning to secure him to the cot. Neither of them could think beyond one step at a time.

Though he moaned, Mohammed remained mercifully unconscious. Blood continued to soak through the makeshift bandages. Akima didn't like the grayish, waxy appearance of his skin. She paused, biting back curses for the Drej; she'd have plenty of time to do that later, probably even the rest of her life.

Standing by the makeshift stretcher on the cluttered street, Akima gazed at the frightened and confused population that had not managed to escape. No one offered to help, as they would have done under other circumstances. She called out, asking for anyone with medical knowledge, but the people scurried off.

For years, Akima's grandmother had taught her to be self-sufficient, to rely on people when necessary, but to find her own solutions if possible.

Akima bent over the cot. "Ready to carry him?"

"Yes, but where are we going?" Ishaq looked around, saw only destruction.

Until this moment, Akima had avoided the question, hoping an idea would magically come to her. She tried to recall any other vessel on New Marrakech that might have gone unnoticed. The Drifter colony itself was composed of old ships, now abandoned and turned into houses, businesses, factories, storage containers. Practically every major building on New Marrakech had once been a spacecraft.

Most of the fleeing refugees had gone to the docking rings to fight over the available starships. But Akima didn't need a ship to carry her a great distance—she only had to break away from the Drifter colony far enough to reach the Solbrecht hospital ship in close orbit overhead.

Her stomach growled, and she realized she hadn't eaten anything in almost a day. Ishaq must be starving as well, but she couldn't take time to secure food now.

Then suddenly, Akima gasped as a possibility occurred to her. The bakery!

Although the colonists came from many faiths and backgrounds on New Marrakech, every neighborhood had a bakery, where families would bring their own dough made at home and place the loaves in the traditional fires. The bakery was a gathering place for conversation, gossip, and news, an Islamic tradition the colonists had adopted because it bound the community together.

Akima had worked at one such bakery off and on for the past two years, and she knew that it was a converted passenger pod, old but intact. Although its interstellar engines had been removed, the hull still retained its integrity, and perhaps the attitude-control thrusters could still function as short-range engines.

She picked up the cot, so excited that she lifted before Ishaq could grasp his end. Fortunately, the strips of cloth kept Mohammed from tumbling off, and they regained their balance, working together. Ishaq didn't question her, seeing the flame of intensity and hope in her eyes. With quick steps, they carried Mohammed through the streets, picking their way over rubble, broken glass, fallen walls.

The bakery was an egg-shaped structure with thick hull plates and studded with large rivets like round candies. The owner of the bakery had whitewashed the corrosion and rust stains on the alloyed hull to disguise the origins of his establishment.

Sturdy flanges held the passenger pod to the main colony framework, but the metal strips wouldn't hold if the small craft's thrusters still worked. As Akima had hoped, everyone had fled the area. She picked up her pace toward the rounded doorway hatch.

Ishaq finally seemed to understand. "You're going to try to fly the bakery?"

"It's a ship. Just like any of these others. I'm pretty sure it'll still function . . . and I think I can fly it."

She remembered the Australian refugees, how they had puttered away from the Drifter colony in a similar passenger pod. She had been uncertain then as to whether they would survive that journey. Akima was just as uncertain now, but that did not stop her.

Inside the elliptical vessel, Akima looked around and called out, but there was no sign of the bakery owner or his family. They set Mohammed down on the metal floor and swung the hatch shut. The long-unused airlock controls glowed green, and Akima heard a hiss of seals. The cargo doors indicated that pressurization was complete.

The fires in the bread oven had been banked down, and Akima closed off the exhaust port. Piled boxes covered what had obviously been spacecraft bulkheads and engine compartments. The smell of flour, yeast, and fresh loaves hung in the air.

On the floor, Mohammed coughed. A fresh burst of

blood trickled from beneath the bandages. Some of his wounds had reopened. When he stopped groaning, Akima was even more worried about him. They didn't have much time left.

She shoved crates aside and climbed a ladder to the upper level, the pod's original cockpit, which now served as the chief baker's administrative office and records storage room. She knocked papers away to expose the spacecraft piloting panel and the captain's chair.

Her heart sank. Few of the pod's controls looked familiar at all. Many systems had been shut down, probably for years, although those that still operated winked green. "All right," she said to herself. "One step at a time."

Akima flicked on the main circuits, trying not to think of how lost she was. She'd watched ships fly, she had talked to pilots. "I can do this," she said, then repeated it, as if that might make it true. But she had hoped the task would be easier.

Ishaq scrambled up the ladder, his face flushed. "I've anchored Father with crash restraints and made him as comfortable as I could."

The boy's lips were trembling, his hands shaking. Akima knew he was on the brink of despair. But she couldn't allow herself to panic now, and she couldn't let Ishaq do it either. She had to give him something to do.

"Find me the manual," she said. "Look up the instructions to make sure we're doing everything right. We'll only get one chance."

Ishaq seized on the instructions, glad to have something useful to occupy himself with. He scrambled through records and called up documentation that explained how the engines worked, how to configure flight protocols, how the controls affected the flight path.

"Here's the troubleshooting guide," he said, then flicked through screen after screen.

Akima found the activation controls and powered them to standby level. She already knew that the heavy, interstellar drives had been intentionally removed, but she didn't need those. They just had to get as far as the hospital ship.

The fuel levels were low, too, but the reactor chamber still contained enough for takeoff . . . or so she hoped. With the punch of a button, she sent a pulse through the attitude-control jets. The bakery vessel trembled, straining against the metal flanges that attached the pod to the ground; as Akima increased power she could hear metal groaning. With all her heart, she hoped the noise came from outside, and not part of their ship.

"All right. There's that one," she said.

Ishaq finally located the controls. "I think I've figured out how to maneuver." He switched on several other panels that glowed brightly.

"Maneuvering is Step Two," Akima said. "*Moving* is my main priority now." She didn't want to think about Mohammed's condition as he lay all alone on the main deck below. "We've got to tear ourselves free of New Marrakech." Urgency built within her until brashly, afraid they were out of time, she punched the thrusters and eased the level as high as it would go.

The bakery vessel shuddered. The attitude jets fired hotter. She heard ripping, screeching metal.

Ishaq, his green eyes wide, scanned the on-line documentation, searching. "Wait!" he cried. "No, no. First you've got to increase the reactive thrust and—"

One of the engines coughed, stuttered, and died. Then

the opposite thruster, blasting unevenly, tilted the vessel, adding too much strain in only one direction. The flange on the left side of the bakery pod snapped free, tearing up base plates and twisting the girders beneath.

While one side of the bakery blasted away, the opposite connecting bars and plates held them in place. Instead of taking off, the bakery pod leaned over and crashed down on its side, flattening abandoned buildings next to it.

Yelling, Akima and Ishaq grabbed on to the cockpit seats, trying to keep themselves from falling as the passenger pod toppled. Crates crashed and bounced all around them; strewn papers fluttered in the air.

Akima lost her grip and tumbled into the boy. Both of them fell roughly to the pod's curved sidewall, which now felt like the floor. The attitude-control thruster continued to burn until, finally, it sputtered out.

They heard groaning metal, and the clanking impact of loose equipment down below. Akima rolled over, letting Ishaq scramble free and race toward the ladder, which was now sideways. He called out his father's name while Akima grabbed for the control panel, even though she knew it was no use.

If she couldn't get the engines started, they had no hope left. When she saw that all the controls were dead, Akima realized she was out of options. She had failed. She'd thought she could fly the ship, a simple passenger pod, but the attempt had ended catastrophically.

Warning lights blinked on the control panel, indicating several hull breaches from the collapse of the bakery. So even if Akima did manage to fire up the engines again and leave New Marrakech, their air would bleed away. They would all die in space.

Knowing she could do nothing to repair the bakery ship now, her thoughts turned to Mohammed.

Akima made her way through the hatch and down into the topsy-turvy main chamber. Mohammed's stretcher had broken loose and been tossed like a piece of flotsam against the warm bakery oven; crates and flour sacks had tumbled in every direction. Ishaq flung the debris away to reach his father. He knelt beside Mohammed, putting an arm around his shoulder, and Akima joined him.

As if sensing their presence, Mohammed regained consciousness for just a few moments. He coughed and looked at them both as his eyes cleared. "Our work," he said with a choke. "Carry on . . ."

And then his lips clenched together as if he meant to say the word *please*. Ishaq held his father gently as he convulsed, then coughed and went still. No first aid could help him now. Mohammed died, leaving them alone on the devastated Drifter colony.

— 7 —

For the next few weeks, Akima's nightmares were full of Drej Stingers glowing with blue fire, ships exploding in midair, and bleeding people reaching out to her for help, though she had none to give. Especially Mohammed. Over and over she relived her failure to pilot the bakery ship. Time and again she heard the grinding crash as the passenger pod fell on its side. . . .

Now, with their home destroyed, Akima and Ishaq were refugees among refugees. They lived in shelters erected from what remained of the dwellings in the Drifter colony, and everyone worked together to put out the fires, sift through the wreckage, and pick up the pieces.

Ishaq had suffered a cut to the left side of his chin, which had begun to heal to a red, ragged scar; Akima's shoulder ached from when the bakery's collapse had thrown her into a cockpit support strut. The cut near her hairline, though almost invisible now, throbbed with dull pain. But she welcomed that pain, preferred it to the emotional misery of knowing that her lack of experience, her inability to defend against or even flee the attack, had made her partly responsible for Mohammed's death.

Thousands of colonists had been lost, and the survivors who had escaped the carnage gradually trickled back to New Marrakech. Meanwhile, Akima and Ishaq worked themselves to exhaustion to provide the most basic medical attention to those who had been injured. They helped fellow Drifters erect temporary shelters and comb through the smashed ruins of shops and homes to salvage usable items. The returning colonists set up distribution areas for the food and medical supplies they had brought back with them.

Even following such a disaster, Akima took comfort in the sharing and sense of community, the willingness to sacrifice that she saw among her fellow Humans—far different from when she and Ishaq had begged for help during the attack. Surely the Drifters represented the best, and occasionally the worst, that humanity had to offer. It gave the two orphans hope, which they needed more than anything at this point.

On their own, Akima and Ishaq went to the wreckage of their former home, extracting trinkets, clothing, padbooks and datapads, and scorched furniture. Miraculously, many of the teaching texts and books showing old Earth had survived.

Scores of funerals cycled through the low-grav dome, where Akima had said farewell to her grandmother. At times, entire families floated in the central area reserved for the dead. Everyone was exhausted from mourning those who had fallen in the unprovoked Drej attack.

There was endless grieving to be done and countless dead to commemorate, so the colonists adapted.

Akima and Ishaq adapted as well. Before long, they began work on the old dwelling where Akima had lived with her grandmother, which was empty now. It needed a great many repairs, but they set to work, Akima scrounging material and fixing systems while Ishaq studied maintenance charts and tried to tell her what parts she needed. Because so few of the former homes were currently habitable, they brought two homeless families into their small dwelling to live with them. They counted themselves lucky to have as much space as they did. Akima and Ishaq shared the room that had formerly belonged to her grandmother.

Strangely, instead of succumbing to despair, they rose to the new challenges. Akima had suffered too much loss in her life: her world destroyed, her family lost, her grandmother and uncle dead, her colony shattered, and her beloved mentor killed. Others might have broken under the strain, but Akima found new strength and determination. She drew on her grandmother's teachings and did what was important *now*.

One day, standing out on the streets of New Marrakech and watching the colonists rebuilding, helping one another, she vowed not only to survive, but to become successful. She would learn from her failures and do everything in her power to ensure that she would not repeat the mistakes of her past.

She wanted to become a pilot—a good one.

Enlisting Ishaq's aid, she gathered padbooks, datapads, and holoscrolls about every kind of space vessel that frequented New Marrakech. After long days of rebuilding homes, unloading and distributing supplies, or delivering food, Akima would study far into the night. Sometimes Ishaq sat beside her, poring over first aid manuals and medical texts, wishing he had taken the time to learn it all sooner. Each time Akima visited a home constructed from a vessel-type that was new to her, she found the cockpit area and familiarized herself with its controls.

When working at the loading docks, Akima spent time with the cargo pilots and even convinced them to let her go on brief supply runs to learn the ropes of flying. Within months, because of the scarcity of experienced pilots, she found herself with a full-time job piloting short-range cargo haulers. She derived great satisfaction from this, knowing that if ever again she was faced with a crisis that required a pilot, she would know what to do. . . .

While Akima studied to become a pilot, Ishaq used his time teaching the students his father had left behind, though he wasn't much older than the class members. Considering Ishaq's youth, Akima was surprised by how seriously he took the job, but his father would have wanted the knowledge to be passed on. Late at night, as Akima memorized vehicle schematics and operating manuals, Ishaq added salvaged history, literature, culture, and mythology texts to his reading. By day, when he was not teaching, Ishaq's time was taken up in his duties as primary chef for the large household.

His reasons for making such a strong effort were not lost on Akima. It mirrored her own determination to become a pilot. They both needed to assuage their guilt over Mohammed's death by ensuring that they would never again be caught unprepared. . . .

Months passed as each of them grew more and more

proficient at their tasks. One evening, after a simple but surprisingly delicious dinner of couscous with spices and bits of meat, Akima sat with Ishaq in their small room. For historical completeness, Ishaq had asked her to write a description of what she remembered about the evacuation of Earth and the founding of the Drifter colonies. Akima jotted down notes on a datapad while Ishaq tinkered with the password-locked holoscroll that his father had died trying to retrieve during the Drej attack.

"He told me this was important, you know." He turned the holoscroll over, but could not decipher it. "He always meant to give me the code to open it when I was old enough." Without success, Ishaq experimented with passwords in various forms and different languages.

Akima winced at the reminder of Mohammed's untimely death. She ran her eyes down her notes. "We always assume we're going to have more time. The truth is, we just don't know. That's why my grandmother believed in doing anything important *now*. At every moment you need to decide what the best use of time is, and then do that."

Ishaq looked up from the holoscroll, cocked his head, and looked at her with his piercing green eyes. "Is that what we're doing now? The most important thing?"

The question jolted her. She drew in a deep, calming breath, let it out slowly. "I . . ." she began. "Until this moment, I thought the most important thing was to help repair the colony, take care of you, and learn to be a pilot."

Ishaq looked at her gravely. "But New Marrakech is well on its way to being rebuilt. We can't contribute much more."

"True," Akima agreed. "And I've already learned

everything I can from piloting simple cargo ships. Not to mention that the spaceport is bringing in five new pilots next week, fresh out of the best schools in the Spiral Arm."

Ishaq brightened. "Maybe you should go to one of those schools. You know, become a real hotshot with good ships, not just cargo haulers. I'd go along, of course, so you wouldn't have to worry about whether I was being taken care of. I bet we could scrape up enough credits for the tuition."

Akima scowled, wondering if he was implying that she wasn't a good enough pilot already. "Not necessary," she said finally. "I'm a fast learner, and I can teach myself anything I need to know about flying. But you're right: we should leave New Marrakech, at least for a while, make a new start."

A flush of excitement warmed her face as an idea came to her. "We could become freelance supply traders. We'll buy an old cargo ship, a cheap one, and I could teach myself to be a better pilot through on-the-job practice. And while we're traveling, we can talk to Humans everywhere we go, and you can learn more about Earth's history."

Ishaq nodded. "Maybe we'll even find people who worked with my father on his part of the Titan Project. They might be able to give me clues about what's in this holoscroll and why he thought it was so important."

Akima tapped an index finger to her lips for a moment. "So we agree then?" she said, dazed at how quickly they had come to this decision.

"You're sure not going to leave me behind," Ishaq said.

"No way." She clasped his hand in hers. "We're partners."

Within three days it was arranged. Akima and Ishaq sold off all unnecessary possessions. They withdrew the credits Akima's grandmother and Mohammed had left in their modest savings accounts. For a small but tidy sum, they sold their current house to the two families who now shared it with them, then placed all the larger cultural artifacts they had salvaged into a long-term storage vault in the heart of the souks.

They purchased a serviceable old freighter from one of the merchant captains at the spaceport—a vessel with which Akima was already quite familiar. Then, using her connections among the cargo pilots, she was able to wrangle their first assignment: making a small cargo delivery to the nearby planet Solbrecht. They received one quarter of the delivery fee up front; the rest of the credits would be deposited into their account with a New Marrakech moneylender after the delivery.

Knowing that the ship was their own gave Akima a sense of pride and independence as she fired up the engines.

Ishaq grinned over at her from the copilot's station. "Ready for takeoff, Captain."

Akima blinked in surprise. In all of her months of piloting cargo ships, no one had ever called her captain. "*Captain* Akima . . . ? I like it."

With that, they blasted away from New Marrakech.

—8—

En route to nearby Solbrecht on their first bona fide business run, Akima practiced the fancier maneuvers that cargo pilots were strictly forbidden to use—flips, loops, waggles, spins. She laughed with delight when each one proved easier than she had anticipated.

With her new piloting skills, Akima believed she and Ishaq would make a fine living with their freighter, christened the *Ronin*. In the days of ancient Japan, a samurai without a master was called a ronin, an itinerant warrior who could fight for whatever cause he chose. Since her grandmother and Mohammed were both dead, and she and Ishaq were now without a "master," the name seemed appropriate. Akima might even be considered a rogue of sorts.

"Don't show off for my benefit." Ishaq sounded unimpressed. "Trick flying in the void between planets is one thing. Pulling these maneuvers in gravity against atmosphere is another challenge completely."

Akima just grinned. "Nothing I can't handle."

After her grandmother's death, she had used a curved samurai sword, a *wakazashi*, to cut her silky black hair. Because the wise old woman would no longer be there to brush the long, thick tresses, Akima had vowed always to keep it short. Recently, she had even dyed the two front strands on either side a bright purple in Mohammed's honor—his favorite color. A whole new start.

She looked through the vessel's front kleersteel port, watching their destination planet grow larger as they approached it. "I bet in a year we'll earn enough credits to get a new ship, something with a lot more power. But the *Ronin* should be perfect for our first few jobs. Alien traders at the New Marrakech spaceport told me that any pilot who's willing to work hard can make a fortune on cargo runs from Solbrecht."

Not that they'd earn much from hauling the two dozen crates of herd-tracking transceiver tags that they now carried in their hold.

"And how will we find these lucrative job opportunities?" Ishaq asked. "We don't know anybody on Solbrecht."

Akima shrugged. "One of the traders gave me a name—Golbus, I think it was—one of the biggest businessmen in the entire Spiral Arm. We could use some quick credits since we spent most of our savings on the *Ronin*."

"Let's stick with one thing at a time," Ishaq said noncommittally. "Coming up on Solbrecht now, so forget about fancy maneuvers and quick credits and just get us safely onto a landing pad. Then we can make our first delivery."

Akima gave him a cool look. "Of course. There's

nothing to worry about, you know. I'm already so used to flying this ship it's almost as easy as walking."

"I hope you're right," Ishaq said. "It looks like the drop-off coordinates your friend gave us aren't near any big spaceports. As a matter of fact, it looks like we're headed toward a hilly area just outside of Zechaat, the capital city." He frowned. "I'm reading pretty high winds."

"Well, you've done your part. Now let me do mine," Akima said with more confidence than she actually felt. When they entered Solbrecht's atmosphere, a heavy jolt sent shudders through the *Ronin*. She swallowed hard and gripped the controls more tightly.

"I got it, I got it," she said in a barely audible voice.

She had just gotten the ship stabilized by the time they plunged into a layer of clouds. Suddenly, they were surrounded by milky-yellow whiteness. Akima could see nothing, and only the *ping* from the landing beacon at their destination told her that she was still headed in the right direction. She didn't like this at all. None of her previous maneuvers had prepared her for such a rough approach.

A gust of harsh wind smacked the ship, as if they had bounced off an invisible wall. The controls jumped in Akima's hands. The *Ronin* spun, and Akima fought to bring it back under control and head it in the right direction—or so she hoped, since she still couldn't see anything.

"Is it supposed to be like this?" Ishaq said, his skin turning a color not dissimilar to the clouds around them. His lips pressed together, as if to bite back a scream. The ship bucked again, then emerged beneath the cloud layer, flying level with the horizon.

Akima shot him a glance. "See? I told you I had it under control." She put the *Ronin* into a gradual descent. But before she could look back out the front viewport—in that split second—a sharp downdraft caught the ship, sending them into a plunge. Akima pulled up on the controls. She tried to say something, but it only came out as, "Ah-ah-ahhh!"

She could hear Ishaq's breath coming in short gasps. "Orders, Captain?" he panted, obviously trying hard to sound calm.

Not wishing to alarm him any further, Akima didn't risk making the *ahhh* noise again. She shook her head and aimed straight for the beacon.

There, she had it.

Just when she was beginning to relax, Ishaq said, "Help!" Or that's what she *thought* he said. A moment later he repeated himself: "Hill! *Hill*!"

Squinting out the front viewport, she quickly realized that the bluish-gray she'd taken for sky was actually a high mound—or very low mountain. She pulled up, up, *up*, and braked their speed. There . . . there was the top. They were going to make it.

But despite her best efforts, the lower hull of the *Ronin* scraped a rocky outcropping. They tumbled over the crest onto the downward slope, then end-over-end, turning and striking the ground with screeching thuds. The *Ronin*'s attitude fins slowed their momentum as they continued to plow down the hillside. Boulders seemed to reach out and grab at them. The small freighter finally came to a precarious stop against a large hummock, showered with mud and dirt.

Fearing the worst, Akima looked over at Ishaq. She remembered with horror her debacle trying to fly the bakery passenger pod, and how she had failed to get Mohammed to the medical help he needed so badly. Panting, Ishaq blinked at her and then nodded. Relief washed over her, and she willed her muscles to unclench.

Akima removed her crash restraints, climbed over to the emergency exit hatch, and pounded on the release lever. The hatch popped free with a loud *thunk-whoosh*.

"Well, you almost hit the drop-off point. It's only a kilometer to the north. Now what?" Ishaq said, scrambling up beside her. He looked at the flickering controls.

She gritted her teeth for a moment, knowing she should apologize, but not yet able to admit defeat. "We . . . uh . . . we assess the damage."

It was extensive. Ishaq groaned as he surveyed the wounded vessel: a ship they had only owned for a few days.

"Some of our cargo is intact, but we'll never get enough credits to make repairs," he observed.

Akima drew a deep breath, willing herself to look on the positive side of the situation as a cold gray rain began sleeting down out of Solbrecht's skies. "Why worry about the ship? We'll look for work, salvage however many of those herd-tracking transceiver tags we can, then make the delivery. I'm sure it won't take very long." She swallowed hard, hoping she had managed to convince the boy. "Besides, we weren't planning on going right back to New Marrakech anyway."

"No," Ishaq agreed, but his face was troubled. Solbrecht seemed gloomy and hostile, not a very welcoming place. "But what if we need to get away from *here*?"

– 9 –

Even after the long walk into the city, Zechaat was hardly a sight for sore eyes. In fact, as Ishaq put it, the capital of Solbrecht was a sight to make the eyes sore. The skyline appeared random and jagged, as if some rampaging giant had broken all the glassware in his home and then tossed the shards into a jumbled heap. No doubt some galactic tourism guide called it "exotic architecture."

The streets themselves were dirty, convoluted, and poorly labeled. When Akima stopped and tried to ask for directions from any of the Solbrecht locals, the four-armed creatures either ignored her or launched into streams of untranslatable epithets before hurrying away.

Akima shook her head in disgust. "I don't get it. I thought Solbrecht was supposed to be a planet with business opportunities at every corner."

Ishaq nudged at a piece of moist, lumpy-looking garbage with the tip of his boot. It roused itself and scurried off, startling him. "I hate to mention it, but maybe we should rethink our plan about finding this Golbus guy and applying for a job. We don't even have enough hard credits in hand to buy ourselves food, much less make repairs to the *Ronin*."

Akima grimaced, looking around but seeing no good prospects. "I thought it was going to be easier than this. People here sure aren't very helpful." She ran a hand through her short black hair. "Okay, let's try to make our delivery, if we can pry it out of the wrecked cargo hold. At least we'll have some credits, and *then* we can look for work."

The two young partners returned to their crashed ship on the outskirts of Zechaat. Nobody had even bothered to come and investigate. Sighing in disgust and working through the damp night, Akima and Ishaq salvaged half of their original shipment.

"There's a lot more here than I first thought." They fought a stiff wind as they worked, but Akima kept up a cheerful, if forced, commentary. "It looks like we'll come out of this okay. I have a feeling that when we look around the ship again, we'll find that there's a lot less damage than we'd guessed at first."

Ishaq grunted and helped Akima load a utility cart with the herd-tracking transceiver tags. He didn't sound convinced as he adjusted the expandable cart to hold more cargo. "Do I dare mention that our hull was breached? We won't be able to carry any shipments until we get that fixed."

"You worry too much, Ishaq. As soon as we make this delivery, I've got it covered. Somebody's sure going to be happy to see these herd tags."

Finally, Ishaq couldn't help but be affected by her

enthusiasm and gave her a reluctant smile. "If you say so, Captain. I'm with you all the way."

With the cart controls on full hover, they managed to wrestle the overloaded cargo carrier to the delivery point inside a ramshackle collection of disreputable-looking structures. Unfortunately, when they arrived at the drop-off building (little more than a low shed above the ground), the place seemed deserted.

Breathing hard, they stepped through the open trapezoidal door. The shed was dim inside, but Akima could see crates of cargo stacked along the walls. A freight lift and a turbo-conveyor belt, presumably leading down to a main storage area underground, were just inside the doorway.

"Hello?" Akima tested. "We have the delivery you're waiting for from New Marrakech."

"Yeah, all the herd-tracking transceiver tags you could possibly want," Ishaq added.

That was when pandemonium broke loose. Blindsided, Akima never saw her attacker until he was on top of her. Ishaq yelled, and then she heard fists smacking into something solid. It took less than a heartbeat for her self-defense instincts to kick in. Her grandmother had trained her in numerous martial arts for just such emergency situations.

In one smooth movement, Akima kicked and rolled so that her assailant was now beneath her. She sprang off and turned to help Ishaq, but two more thugs were already approaching from either side. She grabbed one of the two attackers—luckily, he had an extra set of arms for her to hold. Using his momentum, she threw him into the other, sending them both sprawling to the ground.

"Please! You have made a mistake. We are only attempting to make a delivery of—" Ishaq cried out, but his sentence ended in a grunt of pain.

"No mistake," a voice growled from the dim shadows. "You're Humans and not welcome here. We got orders to make sure you understand that."

The shock of the statement registered on Akima, but she had no time to stop and protest. A gray-skinned arm shot over her shoulder, perhaps in an attempt to strangle her, but she took a firm grasp on it, bent forward, and sent the thug hurtling over her shoulder, legs and four arms flailing in the air. Grunts and shouting sounds came from where Ishaq had been.

Another attacker bounded toward Akima in a flying tackle. As if in slow motion, she noticed an unusual metal badge—inscribed with a double snake-head design—on the thug's right shoulder. The attacker made a grab for Akima's cropped hair and missed by a centimeter when Akima jumped and dove to one side, executed a neat shoulder roll, and sprang back to her feet. *One more reason to keep my hair short*, Akima thought gratefully.

More forms lunged at her from out of the shadows, but Akima was ready for them. She refused to admit defeat.

The attackers, unfortunately, had other ideas.

Every muscle in Akima's body was sore. A fist-sized area on her cheek throbbed, and her flightsuit had been badly torn. Her head felt as if a dozen acrobats had used her skull as a springboard.

Ishaq had not fared nearly as well. Surprised by Akima's ability to fight back, the thugs had fled after a time, but not before two of them had dumped the contents of the cargo cart down the turbo-conveyer and sealed the chute opening. At the same time, three other Solbrecht thugs had dealt a few final blows to Ishaq's already injured body.

"And I thought the crash had to be the worst part of the day," he groaned.

"I think losing our cargo, and all the credits, ranks right up there," Akima said glumly.

"Yeah? It gets worse." In a weak, remote voice, Ishaq summarized his injuries—using the technical terms he remembered from his medical texts—and directed Akima while she bound the swollen gash at his ribs and splinted the break in his leg. For a moment, guilt threatened to overwhelm her for having brought the boy into such a dangerous situation. She quickly squelched the useless emotion. *Now.* What was important *now*?

Akima turned the cargo cart upright and examined it. "Nothing broken." She glanced at Ishaq's fractured leg, then looked away. "At least not here. We can make it back into town." She helped the boy onto the sled, adjusted the hover controls, and pushed the cart out through the open door.

Though Ishaq weighed significantly less than their lost cargo, the cart was now less stable in the gusting wind as they made their way into Zechaat. Akima had to keep a firm grip on the handles, needing all of her strength to keep the cart from capsizing and dumping Ishaq to the ground. Once they reached the streets in the jagged capital city, the buildings acted as a windbreak.

For two hours, Akima tried unsuccessfully to find a doctor to treat Ishaq. "This is an emergency!" she said, but her pleas were ignored—especially since they had no credits on hand to offer for payment.

Gritting her teeth, Akima forced herself to go on. "No wonder they call them 'the mean streets of Solbrecht,' " she muttered, driving the hovercart around a corner to start up a narrow avenue. "Doesn't anybody care?" she shouted to anyone who would listen.

"Whoa, whoa!" a sharp voice replied from the side of the thoroughfare. "I care that you learn how to steer that thing."

Startled, Akima looked up into the pointed face of a Mantrin female whose balled fists were planted firmly on her hips. At least Akima *thought* she was a Mantrin, judging from her huge legs and long, slashing tail. She'd met only one before, since few visited Human Drifter colonies. To Akima, they looked like gigantic, intelligent kangaroos with exaggerated arms, triple-jointed legs, yellow eyes, and fearsomely sharp teeth set in a narrow, beaklike face.

Akima was long past the point of being afraid for herself. Ishaq's injuries concerned her most at the moment. "Look, I promise I'll learn how to steer if you help me find a doctor for my friend. We were attacked while trying to make a delivery."

"Uh-huh," the alien said, but she unclenched her fists and leaned over to examine Ishaq. She cocked her head, gestured for Akima to follow, and ducked into a small alley. "On second thought," she said, reappearing a moment later. "You'd better let me do that." The big Mantrin grabbed the cart handles from Akima and pushed it into the alley.

Akima wanted to ask where they were going, but something told her she could trust this alien, no matter how dangerous she appeared. At one point, the Mantrin paused, turned back to Akima, and said merely, "Stith."

Ishaq stared, befuddled, then Akima answered, "Akima. My name is Akima. He's Ishaq."

Their benefactor, Stith, paused at the rear doorway to a building, then punched a code on a keypad. Doors swished aside and a ramp extruded. Akima followed the plodding alien and the hovercart up the ramp. Once inside the well-lit storage area, Stith sealed the doors again. "Hey, Jemfuh!" she called.

A portly four-armed Solbrechtian waddled into the room. "Stith! Uh, always a pleasure doing business with you." He had a wary look on his gaunt, gray face. "A *risk* these days, but also a pleasure."

"Look, I need some medical supplies to treat my Human friend here." Stith's triangular yellow eyes fixed Jemfuh with a piercing gaze. "No questions asked." Thinking fast, Akima rattled off all the items she thought they might need. Stith made several additions while Jemfuh scribbled notes on a datapad, using his lower-left hand. He nodded.

The Solbrechtian shot Stith a questioning look. "If I get all of this, how will it affect my account?"

Stith considered. "I'll write off a third of your debt, not a credit more."

From the look of delight on the four-armed alien's face, Akima decided he must have owed a lot of credits to Stith. Jemfuh spun and left the room with a positive spring in his step.

"He's sort of a local herbalist," Stith explained. "A bit mercenary, too, but he's a good guy. We'll be safe here." With muscular arms, Stith lifted Ishaq gently onto a workbench, made a careful examination of his head, limbs, and torso, muttering and grumbling to herself.

"I'll find a way to pay you back," Akima said.

"What did you do to make these people mad at you, anyway?" Stith asked.

"We don't even know who they were." Akima told Stith everything that had happened since their arrival on Solbrecht. When she got to the part about the emblem with the double snake-head, Stith growled.

"*Golbus?* You had to make an enemy out of Golbus? That's all we need. Most powerful crime lord in the Spiral Arm, and you decide to tick him off?"

Just then, the herbalist scuttled in with a trayload of medical supplies, placed them on the workbench beside Stith, and scuttled back out. By now, Ishaq had slipped into unconsciousness.

"Golbus? A *crime* lord? And I was thinking of asking him for a job," Akima said. "But we've never even met. How could I have done something to make him angry with me?"

Stith hunched a muscular shoulder in a one-sided shrug. "With Golbus? Doesn't take much. He hates Humans just on general principles, because he's terrified of the Drej." While Akima applied salve and a poultice to Ishaq's open wound, Stith assisted; apparently the basics of first aid were the same, regardless of species. "I managed to tick him off myself. Golbus has all twenty fingers into every sort of business you can name, including illegal ones."

"And something you did upset him?" Akima said.

Stith grunted. "More like something I *didn't* do. Until a few days ago, I was primarily an arms dealer, traded in exotic weapons. Wasn't a huge business, but as successful as they come around these parts. I'm a specialist.

I know weapons. Sometimes I even took in students, if the price was right and the deals were legal. Did business with Golbus a couple of times, too, but only on things that were totally aboveboard.

"Then he got greedy, tried to strong-arm me into selling him armaments at a discount . . . in exchange for his 'benevolent protection.' When I didn't knuckle under, Golbus destroyed my business, burned my shop, and left me with only a couple of fancy handweapons I was carrying at the time." She waved one clawed hand to indicate holsters at her shoulders and waist, which held amazingly wicked-looking blasters and disrupters.

"All that, just because you stood up to him?" Akima said. "That's bad."

Stith gave a bark that sounded like a harsh laugh. "You got a talent for understatement, you know? Don't worry about me too much. I'll land on my feet. With my skills, I can get a good job just about anywhere. And, as soon as I teach Golbus a little lesson and get off this planet, I *will*."

"I don't need to teach anyone a lesson," Akima said, "except maybe myself. But I'd sure like to get off of Solbrecht. Unfortunately, our ship is damaged, and we don't have the credits to repair it."

Moving with military efficiency, Stith set the broken bone and applied an instrument that looked like a tuning fork to the region of the injury. Ishaq's eyes fluttered open, and Stith spoke to him. "There, good as new— well, almost. Just don't put much weight on that leg for a couple days." She looked at Akima. "Tell you what, why don't we throw in together? I've been itching to leave this place, but Golbus has me stuck. I help you find a way to get your ship fixed, you help me get off Solbrecht."

"Deal," Akima said. "But with Golbus angry at us, it'll be tough to get the supplies we need and the credits to pay for the ship repair."

Stith gave her a sharp-toothed grin. "Oh, I've got a few ideas on how to get around that."

—10—

Weak, but vastly improved, Ishaq looked from Stith to Akima, his face pinched with concern over the crazy plan. "But aren't you afraid of Golbus? He's the . . . the big guy around here."

Stith made a loud snort and thrashed her thick tail in annoyance. "Everyone's afraid of Golbus. That's exactly why this scheme will work."

They sat in front of the damaged *Ronin* spaceship, which had been towed from the crash site to the salvage dock. Cold, gray rain spat at them from the skies.

Throughout the afternoon, Akima had turned away numerous curiosity seekers, finally convincing them that the wreckage was not for sale. When pesky scavengers had tapped the *Ronin*'s scratched hull, scrutinizing it, Stith, with her massive legs and growling disposition, had chased them off.

Looking at the damage the freighter had suffered during their rough crash landing, Akima was amazed at

Stith's confidence that it could be repaired. They certainly didn't have the credits to pay for it in any conventional fashion, but she was proud of the ingenious and satisfyingly humorous plan she and Stith had concocted. Besides, she and Ishaq didn't have much to lose—not if they ever wanted to get off of Solbrecht.

The muscular alien hunched over and turned her yellow gaze first to Ishaq, then to Akima. "Ready?"

Akima pressed a finger to her lips for a moment, then nodded. "It's nothing I can't handle. I'll do my part if you'll do yours."

Ishaq swallowed a lump in his throat. "I'm perfectly happy to stay here and keep recuperating." He held up the code-locked holoscroll they had taken from his father's dying grasp. "Maybe I can figure this thing out after all."

Stith made a rumbling sound deep in her throat. "Just make sure you keep those pack-rat scavengers away from the ship. There'd better be a vessel here for the repair crews to fix once we convince them to come our way."

The starship repair dock owned by Ringus the Refurbisher was well-known as the most expensive, most elite, engine overhaul facility on Solbrecht. It was also a front for servicing ships for the crime lord Golbus. Ringus specialized in the removal of incriminating markings and identification numbers on stolen craft.

With her rolling gait, Stith marched through the giant blast hatches and walked across the banging and welding chaos in the repair bay. Numerous aliens worked in and around wrecked space yachts that had been stolen or lost in gambling games. Some of the creatures belonged to species with an intuitive grasp of interstellar mechanics and starship operations; other creatures, Stith believed, should have been legally restrained from ever picking up a wrench or electrospanner.

She strode along with thundering footsteps, her tail lashing from side to side, her pointed mouth clamped tightly shut. She had to appear as if she knew what she was doing, and Stith was certainly capable of fostering the proper impression. She went directly to Ringus's offices, jostling a few intimidated managers out of the way.

She burst through the corrugated door without knocking, startling the master of the repair shop. Her palms stung from slapping the ridged metal, but it felt good, too. She flexed her fingers, sheathing and unsheathing her claws. "Ringus! I have a ship that needs to be repaired. Right now. High priority."

The rodentlike creature with large ears who sat next to Ringus the Refurbisher started sniggering uncontrollably. The creature barely stood as tall as Stith's waist, and she could have squashed him into goo with one flick of her tail. When she glared at the rodent, he let out a terrified squeak and dashed behind a heavy piece of office furniture.

The gaunt repair master sat up, his round amber eyes widening in amusement or annoyance. "I don't take orders from you." He sniffed the air, as if Stith exuded a particularly sour stench. "But I do ask questions. First, who do you think you are? Second, what gives you the right to demand priorities in my shop? And third, even if I agree, how do you intend to pay for repairs?"

For her answer, Stith removed a medallion emblazoned with the double snake-head from her belt, a trinket

Golbus and his thugs had left as his calling card when they had trashed her weaponry shop. "Answers all three questions, doesn't it, Ringus?"

Startled, Ringus sat back and regarded her with greater gravity. "It's a start," he said. "But I've never heard anything about this before. Golbus has me doing a handful of jobs right now, and he says they're all high priority."

"None higher than this." Stith handed him a printed address that identified the salvage dock to which they had dragged the wreckage of Akima's ship. "Orders straight from the top. We need this craft repaired as soon as possible, within a day at the latest."

Stith balanced on her curved hind legs. Her tail, not unintentionally, smacked the side of the office furniture behind which the rodent creature had hidden. She hoped the clang made his ears ring.

With a growl of his own, Ringus the Refurbisher gestured through the windowports to a space yacht loaded up on suspensors, where a crew was busy overhauling the engine and replacing hull plates. "You see that craft? She'll be beautiful one day. My own private vessel. I've got six mechanics scheduled to work on that baby. Pretty soon I'll have a ship that's the envy of Solbrecht. You're telling me I have to remove my overtime crew in order to fix some wreck of yours?"

Stith shrugged. "You want to argue with Golbus? Be my guest." She slapped the medallion down on the cluttered desk for good measure. The double-headed snake glared up at the repair master.

Then Stith got an idea. A wonderful idea.

"However," she said, approximating a smile with her armored lips, "Golbus rewards those who serve him well. Likes to provide incentives. I'm authorized to let you take workers from any of Golbus's other vessels currently in your shop. Use them to repair my ship, then assign a full-time crew to revamping your own yacht. Spare no expense. Just put it on Golbus's tab."

She thrashed her tail again, banging the office furniture a second time. The rodentlike creature gave an offended squeak. "You've done a good job for Golbus all these years, Ringus. You deserve a reward."

The Refurbisher sat up, surprised. "He's never done anything but complain before, no matter how hard I work my crews."

"Well, that's just his way. You know Golbus," Stith said with a shrug.

Ringus nodded. "Yeah, he has to stay tough if he's going to run the criminal underworld in this sector. But I've always suspected Golbus had a soft heart—a small one—inside there somewhere."

Stith snatched the medallion back, just in case she needed it for another bluff. "So you'll send a repair crew over then?"

"My best mechanics, and all the materials you need," Ringus answered. "We'll make this ship something you can be proud of."

"Make it something that works," Stith said, and stalked out.

Back at the ship, hoping for some peace and quiet after their frantic days, Ishaq didn't mind being alone. It gave him a chance to concentrate on his father's code-locked holoscroll. Ishaq knew it contained a vital secret, but he didn't know what it might be, or how to get to it.

After working with Mohammed for so many years, he

knew the passions that drove his father, knew the work he had done on the Titan Project. Mohammed Bourain and his team had heroically rescued prime examples of Earth art, culture, and history—and they would have been very cautious with such treasures. His father would not have dared to allow unscrupulous beings to get hold of them—especially not the Drej, who would be eager to obliterate the achievements of humanity.

On the other hand, his father would want to make sure that the treasure trove would be found when Earth's refugees had a new world where they could settle or a central gathering place for humankind. For a decade, Mohammed had waited to hear from Sam Tucker. From Captain Korso, Akima had retrieved the last log entries of the great Human scientist . . . but the Drej attack and Mohammed's death had prevented them from using those records in any way.

Ishaq turned the holoscroll over in his hand, trying to find the proper key, something that would unlock it and allow him to read the data inside. All he needed was the name of a planet, the coordinates, the hiding place of Earth's cache of cultural treasures.

He thought of his father and tried password after password, familiar words, places, dates. Ever since the Drej attack on New Marrakech, Ishaq had been keying in everything he could think of, and he remained stumped.

He knew his father must have locked the solution under a code phrase that someone should have been able to figure out, given enough time . . . and no one knew the man better than his own son did.

"Why can't I think of it?" he said, rubbing his eyes.

Then he heard a scratching and clanging noise outside the ship. Favoring his healing leg, Ishaq hurried outside to find a group of scavengers with tiny, quick paws, using tools to dismantle the *Ronin*'s hull plates.

"Hey, get away from there!" he shouted.

The scavengers looked up in alarm. Ishaq ran at them, limping slightly and waving his hands. "This ship is still owned. It's not marked for dismantling," he yelled.

"Well, it should be," one of the scavengers squeaked.

"Go on! Get out of here!" Ishaq kept waving his arms, and the creatures scurried off. Frazzled and flustered, he climbed back into the ship, sat down, and propped his throbbing leg up. He needed to relax so that he could think clearly.

When Ishaq and his father had shared mint tea and baklava or other pastries, Mohammed often played soothing music, classical pieces from old Earth composers. His favorite had always been Mozart, and they would sit together and play *Eine Kleine Nachtmusik, The Marriage of Figaro, The Abduction from the Seraglio*, his *Requiem* mass, *The Magic Flute*, or one of Mozart's many symphonies. With a lump in his throat, Ishaq remembered his father telling him that he believed Wolfgang Amadeus Mozart was the best the Human race had to offer when it came to music.

Ishaq heaved a long sigh, then sat up with a jerk. Mozart! Would he have used that as a password?

He scrambled to retrieve the holoscroll, turned it on and input the name "Mozart." But that was too simple, and the scroll denied the password again. Yet Ishaq knew he was on the right track. Instead, he input musical notes, key sequences from Mohammed's favorite pieces, a virtually unguessable code, but an ingenious solution for anyone who knew the man.

Ishaq guessed it on the third try, a brief passage from

the "Kyrie" of Mozart's *Requiem*. Appropriate, a requiem for planet Earth.

The holoscroll's data display shimmered, then the password lock dissolved and the information revealed itself. Ishaq grinned, seeing the planetary coordinates and the name of the world where Mohammed and his Titan team had hidden the greatest treasures of Human art and culture, rescued just in time before the destruction of Earth: Fauldro, located in a not too distant system. The *Ronin* could easily reach the planet—if Akima and Stith could ever get it fixed.

Feeling warm inside, Ishaq sat back in his worn chair, smiling hugely. Now, at last, they knew a place to go.

At the fueling station that serviced most spaceships in Zechaat, Akima stood with one hand on her hip, waited too long, then raised her voice to get someone's attention. Finally, one of the service aliens shambled up to her on a cluster of rootlike foot tentacles. She had to look at the creature for some time before she could decipher the location of its face and mouth.

"Hey, I need to charge up a ship," she said. "Highest quality fuel, and top off all the tanks." Akima held out a placard that displayed the original make and model of her freighter. She didn't dare let the refuelers see images of what the *Ronin* actually looked like now, after the crash. She just hoped they could get the ship repaired before long.

But that was Stith's job to worry about. Akima just had to obtain the chemicals to run the engines.

The service alien snatched the placard with one flexible tendril and held it close to a pus-green membrane that must have been its eye. "Fill that guzzler full of fuel? Do you know how much it'll cost?" The creature made a strange burbling sound that Akima could only interpret as a rude snort.

"The cost is none of my business," Akima said tersely. "And if you're looking for trouble about this, you can call Golbus right now." She let the name hang in the air.

"Golbus?" The service alien drew back, its hair tentacles trembling like dry leaves wavering in a wind.

"I assume his credit's good," Akima said. "Golbus does have an account with your refueling station?" She raised her eyebrows, waiting.

When the refueling creature didn't answer immediately, Akima pursed her lips. "Hmmm. Maybe I've made a mistake. Perhaps I should suggest that Golbus withdraw all business from your establishment. In fact, he could recommend that others do so as well."

The creature made a high-pitched hum, obviously knowing just how much damage it would cause his business if he were blacklisted by the powerful crime lord. "But you're . . . *Human*. The Drej should've killed you all at once. Nobody cares about Humans."

"I do," Akima said. Then she took out a datapad and began looking around, jotting down notes.

"This is highly irregular," the service alien said. Its body core of flickering roots and tentacles quivered.

Akima continued to scrawl the name of the establishment and its address. "What is your business number, please? I need to include it in my report to Golbus."

The creature shuddered and stammered, its sickly green eye membrane pulsing in alarm. "Wait, wait! That is not necessary."

"Golbus prefers businesses to cooperate when his

name is invoked," Akima said, her voice deep and threatening. "You, sir, are being most *un*helpful, and I think Golbus should know about it."

"No, no, please excuse me. I apologize." All of the service alien's tentacles rose up in the air. "Just tell me where to deliver the fuel. You'll have the highest quality, I assure you, and all you could possibly need. I'll make sure your lubricant tanks are topped off, and even restock your food supplies. Your ship will lack for nothing!"

Akima stopped writing on her datapad. "That's better." She strutted out, wondering if the tentacled alien had any experience in reading Human emotions. If so, he would have spotted her smug and delighted grin.

When Akima and Stith finally met back at the repair bay, they were astonished to find Ishaq seated outside the ship in a comfortable, heated recliner surrounded by drinks and exotic refreshments, with soft music playing. A veritable army of workers crawled over the *Ronin*, attaching hull plates, polishing seams, replacing seals, installing new engine components.

"Looking good," Stith said. "Makes you feel all warm inside, doesn't it?"

Impressed, Akima climbed the boarding ramp and marched into the ship. She saw gleaming chairs, newly upholstered cushions, reproductions of classic Sinjax artwork on the walls, glowing indicator lights, and banks of new cabinets. She hurried back out and gave Ishaq a conspiratorial wink.

"Hey," Akima called, "don't forget to check out all the safety systems."

One of the workers snapped to attention. "I'll get right on it."

Ishaq gestured to the rear compartments. "They've also stocked us up with expensive food supplies, water, an entirely new navigation library, entertainment disks, everything we could want."

"That Golbus sure is quite a guy," Stith said. When she spoke the name of the crime lord out loud, everyone in the hangar bay froze for an instant, then went back to work with renewed energy.

Ringus the Refurbisher strode up to Stith. "My crew is nearly finished. I've put in hundreds of labor hours, and I think you'll be more than satisfied with the finished product."

"Certainly," Stith said, her tail thrashing from side to side. "Did you include plenty of weapons aboard, full stockpile, a wide range of selections?"

"But of course," Ringus said. "We know exactly what Golbus requires."

Stith drew herself up, immensely pleased.

"And my own vessel is proceeding as well," Ringus continued. "I wish to thank Golbus for his generosity."

"Well, finish the work first before you get all mushy about it," Stith said. "Golbus doesn't like to be distracted until a job's done."

"But of course." Ringus hurried back, shouting at his crew to work even faster.

Ishaq nodded toward the *Ronin*, where the repair creatures had begun packing up their tools. The fuel-supply vessel was almost done filling the reaction containers of the newly repaired ship. "We'd better be ready to go as soon as they're finished," the young man said.

Akima muttered out of the corner of her mouth, "Golbus isn't going to be very happy about this."

"My heart *bleeds* for the poor crime lord," Stith said darkly.

While napping at his cluttered desk in his administration office, Golbus sweated through a horrific nightmare about the Drej. He was not pleased when the communication signal woke him up and startled him into questioning whether they were truly under attack from the glowing blue aliens.

"Yes, what is it?" he snapped, surprised to see his repair master, Ringus, appear on the image screen.

The Refurbisher wore an expression of clear pleasure and delight, and he clasped both sets of hands together in deep thanks. "Lord Golbus, I just wanted to pass along my gratitude. You are a being of few kind words, but your generosity is overwhelming. Thank you for your continued business in my establishment, and for allowing me to finish my vessel at your own expense. It would be my greatest honor if you came down to the repair docks and let me show you what all your credits have bought."

Still shuddering from his nightmares about Drej, Golbus was confused before he became angry. "What are you talking about, Ringus? Can't you see I'm busy. Leave me alone." Then the import of the words sank in. "What do you mean, *at my expense*? What have all my credits bought? I've had no contact with you in months."

"I respect your privacy, sir, but my new space yacht is completed, and it will become a treasure of Solbrecht. I have also satisfactorily finished the repairs to the Mantrin weapons merchant's ship, as you ordered. The cost was enormous, as I had feared, but now the whole sector will recognize your good taste and appreciation for quality."

Golbus simmered with anger, still not comprehending the Refurbisher's words. Gradually the meaning became clear. Golbus clenched his four hands in front of him as if strangling the perpetrators of this hoax. At last, he flew into such a rage that most of his assistants fled the building, lest he take out his revenge on inappropriate lifeforms.

Akima flew the *Ronin* better this time. She severed all of the docking restraints from the repair bay while Stith worked the copilot controls. Ishaq kept an eye out through the kleersteel ports.

"Here they come!" he shouted.

Golbus himself strode at the head of a phalanx of his henchmen, all four hands balled into fists. His armed thugs looked ready to tear the ship apart with their bare tentacles, hands, or claws.

Akima eased fuel into the thruster jets. "Time to say goodbye."

The *Ronin* raised up. Golbus staggered back, covering his amber eyes, while the henchmen ran forward as if they meant to grab on to the vessel and hold it down by brute force. But the engines on the newly repaired freighter operated at peak performance. All systems were optimal—and then some.

The henchmen dropped to their knees and withdrew hand weapons, firing and firing at the *Ronin*, but their aim was as bad as their dispositions.

Akima punched the thrusters and the ship launched itself out of the salvage dock. Streaking at full speed away from Solbrecht, they left Golbus and his men behind, eating the backwash of fume-filled air.

—11—

Space stretched behind them, a vast distance growing greater by the moment. With Stith by her side at the *Ronin*'s controls, Akima felt safer by the minute. When Solbrecht and the threat of the crime lord's forces dwindled to a bright dot behind them, she began to laugh at the scam they had pulled.

Ishaq cleared his throat and spoke from behind them. "I kinda hate to mention this, but we never really discussed where we were going."

"Away from Solbrecht," Stith said.

He chuckled. "I mean other than that."

Akima lounged back in the slick new pilot seat Ringus the Refurbisher had installed. "It's about time to decide what our best move would be."

Ishaq grinned, anxious to tell them something. "I've found where we—"

"Whoa, whoa," Stith said, dominating the conversation like an armored land vehicle. "Exactly who is 'we'? Let's set some ground rules first."

Akima looked expectantly at her. "Okay, shoot."

A dangerous glint appeared in Stith's triangular yellow eyes. "First rule: Never, *ever*, say 'shoot' to a weapons specialist."

Akima nodded, trying to look nonchalant. "Okay, but before you go adding rules, remember that we all have our own priorities. We need to be able to make decisions that make sense for ourselves."

Stith grunted. "Fair enough. How 'bout this for Rule Two, then: We put all major decisions to a vote. Any one of us wants out—at any time, for any reason—the others will accept that decision without challenging it."

Akima's independent streak toughened inside her. "Right. Always good to have an escape hatch."

"Fine," Ishaq said quickly, sounding breathless. "And let me suggest Rule Three."

"Sure, kid. What is it?" Stith said.

"In an emergency, the three of us cover *each other's* backs first. Then we help outsiders."

"I can live with that," Akima said, tapping a finger thoughtfully to her lips. She understood that her friend's suggestion also stemmed from the deep pain he still felt over his father's death. Because so many colonists had fled New Marrakech during the Drej attack, without a thought for Ishaq or Akima, there had been no hope of getting Mohammed to medical attention.

"Makes good strategic sense," Stith said. "But if we're going to be depending on each other for our lives, both of you are going to need more training in self-defense." Akima started to object, but Stith cut her off. "*Especially* with weapons."

Akima swallowed her argument. If Golbus's thugs had been armed against her at the cargo drop-off shack, she would have been lost, even with the best martial arts techniques. She looked down at her navigation console. "I'll agree, but could we at least decide where we're going first?"

"As a matter of fact, I've got one suggestion," Ishaq said. "It's a long shot, but I think this could be really important. I broke through a first-level encryption on my father's holoscroll."

Akima yelped with surprise. "You've been working on that for weeks!"

"I've just got the name of a planet, and there seems to be another code to give the exact location of the storage unit." Ishaq looked at the big Mantrin weapons specialist, suddenly uneasy.

Stith turned in the copilot's seat and fixed him with her baleful yellow eyes. "Trust me, kid, I'm no Human-hater. And once I'm somebody's friend, I would never, ever betray them. That's my *personal* code."

"Thanks," Ishaq said in a quiet voice. "I already knew that, but it helps to hear you say it. Anyhow, back on Earth my father worked on the Titan Project, CD—Cultural Division. He and his team rescued priceless, important items of Human culture just before the Drej came, and they hid them in a safe place." He held up the holoscroll. "This says it's on a world called Fauldro."

Akima mulled this over. "I've heard of it, I think. Famous as a long-term storage facility and archive. The administrators there pride themselves on absolute confidentiality."

"Well, if it makes your decision any easier," Stith

chimed in, "Fauldro is also home to one of the best piloting schools in the Spiral Arm. Now that you've got a brand new ship, you could use instruction from some real pros. We've got enough credits."

A hot flush crept into Akima's face at the implication.

"No offense, pal," Stith hurried on. "You're an okay pilot for being self-taught, but you're no match for all the geographic and atmospheric conditions a cargo jockey needs to fly. Nothing wrong with a little help to become the top in your field." Stith paused a moment to let this sink in. "Me, *I* take every opportunity to learn from someone who's better than me."

Akima made a fist. After all, the crash landing on Solbrecht had been her own fault, a result of her unwillingness to listen to advice. "Fauldro it is, then," she agreed. "I'll enter the Flight Academy, and don't be surprised if I turn out to be the best student they've ever had."

Ishaq gave a whoop of delight. "This is going to be great."

"I've got some contacts there, you know," Stith said. "I should be able to find us a little work as soon as we arrive."

"Okay . . ." Akima said slowly, remembering what Golbus's henchmen had said when they had tried to deliver their cargo of herd tags. "And how do the locals feel about Humans?"

"Humans aren't overly popular on Fauldro," Stith admitted. "You're gonna find that a lot. This isn't a nice, safe little Drifter colony, you know. But that shouldn't stop you from getting admitted to the piloting school."

"*Nothing* is going to stop me," Akima said.

"Just to hedge our bets," Stith said, "why don't we

make a little stop and get started on your weapons training? Amblin II is on the way, a pretty much deserted
planet, but the gravity's almost exactly the same as
Fauldro's, and it has atmosphere . . . well, a little, anyway. You'll need breathers, but that shouldn't affect
what I'm gonna teach you."

With the utmost care, just to show how good she could
be, Akima landed the *Ronin* lightly on Amblin II, on a
flat, rock-strewn plain.

"I know the place isn't very pretty," Stith said, fixing
a breather mask over her beaked snout, "but we don't
need pretty for our purposes. Nobody'll care if you shoot
up this place."

Akima and Ishaq, also in breather masks, followed the
Mantrin's lurching gait out onto the desolate surface.
"Thanks to our friend Golbus, we have plenty of weap-
ons for you to train us on," Akima said.

Stith thumped the dirt with her thick tail for emphasis.
"Let's start with these. Pretty basic blaster technology."
She handed them each a weapon from her holsters, and
the lesson began. . . .

After practicing for half a day, Akima was improving.
She took aim at a rock shard a hundred meters away and
blasted it to smithereens.

"Great, kid! You are a natural," Stith said.

Akima felt a warm glow from the praise. "Don't
worry, I'll get even better."

"I've only had two other students—of *any* species—
who ever learned this much in such a short time," Stith
said matter-of-factly. "That's not flattery, it's just the
truth."

"Let me guess," Ishaq said, looking down at all of the

unscathed targets he had *tried* to hit. "I'm not one of those two?"

They had all come to the conclusion by now that Ishaq could not hit the bright side of a moon, but at least he was now familiar with how the weapon functioned.

"Ah, it's okay, kid. You'll get the hang of it," Stith said. "I mean, you got one of the best teachers, so you're bound to learn something."

Ishaq sighed, looking down at his blaster. He fired again at a rock, and missed. "Well, I may not be much of a shot with a blaster, but I'm a pretty decent medic by now, and I know a lot about Earth culture. Once we get to Fauldro, I'll learn even more."

Stith clicked her sharp mouth together. "I get the message, kid. Just a couple more rounds and we'll be on our way."

—12—

Because Akima had long since stopped expecting anything to go smoothly, she was surprised at how quickly Stith managed to obtain work on Fauldro: cleaning, cataloging, and reconditioning old-model blasters for a used-arms dealer.

Akima submitted her application for the prestigious Flight Academy and within a week, she was enrolled and beginning classes.

For her, flying was easy—making friends was the difficult part. Since their famed storage facilities were open to any race with the right amount of credits, Fauldro was a melting pot of many cultures, and although the locals weren't exactly welcoming to Humans, at least they weren't overtly hostile either.

However, since she was the only Human in the school, Akima often bore the brunt of her classmates' joking, which she tried not to take personally. She supposed it had something to do with the "hotshot thing" since, day after day, every Fauldro trainee was under pressure to perform or be pushed out of the system. When they told their jokes, stupid as they were, she didn't let it get under her skin, but gave back as good as she got.

"How many Humans does it take to change a phosphor tube?" one of her fellow students, a Gulcrecian, asked an Akrennian.

"How many?" the Akrennian asked.

"Only one," the Gulcrecian said, twitching its snout-trunk, "but afterward the tube is sure to crash and burn."

"Well, you guys seem to be the experts on crashing and burning," she said, commenting on their previous day's performance.

When she repeated their surly jokes to Stith and Ishaq over dinner back in the *Ronin*, Stith growled, clacking her beak. Ishaq only chuckled, chewing a mouthful of tender meat cooked in honey. "Wow—do they have a surprise coming once you start flying against them."

"He's right, Akima," Stith agreed. "You could say it's a moral imperative to teach those self-styled hotshots a bit of a lesson about what Humans are made of."

"Exactly." Ishaq beamed, returning from the galley and setting a platter of chopped, unidentifiable vegetables in the center of the mess table. "And you don't need to sink to their level, either."

Akima laughed and rolled her eyes. "I know, I know. I'm a pilot now. I can afford to take the high road. I'll just consider it part of the challenge."

"I've got a challenge, too," Ishaq said. "Tomorrow, I'm going to the warehouse district where off-worlders make most of their deposits, to see if I can find any information about what my father stored or where."

For days he had searched through databases, hoping to find clues about Mohammed's priceless stockpile of Earth's cultural treasures. Unfortunately, most of Fauldro's records were strictly confidential. Nobody knew where anything was stored in the vast labyrinth-grid of storage cubicles. But Ishaq intended to look.

Stith tore into a big chunk of meat. "The weapons business is the perfect place to keep an ear out for any trouble. You know the old saying, 'Advance intelligence is worth more than a warehouse full of weapons.' " She shrugged her muscular shoulders. "Of course, I'm glad we have plenty of firearms, too." Stith's big knees stuck up as high as her head at their low dinner table.

Akima flopped back on one of the cushions. "I'm ready for anything those flyboys throw at me."

The instructors at flying school threw plenty at her the next day. All first year students were assigned to simulators that morning, simulators so advanced that each one cost more than three assault-class Alyan Spacejumpers. Each station could emulate a thousand of the most commonly used vessels in the Spiral Arm.

As she took a seat in her assigned simulator, Akima heard the Gulcrecian say in his snuffling voice, "Training Human pilots—what a *waste* of state-of-the-art equipment."

That day the school chancellor, Jaxor, stood at the edge of the simulator room, observing the new batch of students. Akima heard him reply to the Gulcrecian in a low voice that was apparently not intended for her ears, "Of course it's a waste, my friend. I have no time for Humans myself, but our school charter prohibits species discrimination. Even against *Humans*. We can only eliminate students based on lack of talent or ability." The chancellor—who was also an important businessman on Fauldro—gave a raspy, unpleasant laugh. "Of course, there might still be some hope in that area." The Gulcrecian laughed too.

Strapping herself into the simulator, Akima muttered, "Oh, yeah? We'll see about that."

Throughout the day, students flew at the controls of seventeen different simulated vessels. They were given no advance warning of which models they would be expected to fly, and the control panels in front of them changed at random intervals. The trainees were expected to make the mental shift and adapt to the new vessel without any "damage" to cargo or passengers, regardless of the simulated flying conditions: from electromagnetic storms, to heavy gravity, to atmospheric turbulence, to obstacle-strewn space.

As the day wore on, the challenges grew more difficult. Akima never missed a beat. By the end of the session, every student had crashed and burned at least once, but Akima had lasted the longest.

As she stumbled exhausted and exhilarated from her simulator pod, she noticed that some of the students who had been making jokes at her expense refused to meet her eyes. One tall, ethereal alien—a student named Dhornan—gazed at her with reluctant admiration; looking like a salamander furred with mossy outgrowths on moist skin, he seemed silent and brooding. Dhornan's simulator scores were remarkable, too, and Akima couldn't tell if he meant to congratulate her, or if he saw her as a deadly rival. . . .

While Akima was busy proving her worth in the simulator, Ishaq found himself feeling about as lost as he had ever felt. What in the Spiral Arm had he ever been thinking?

He had made his way to the warehouse district reserved primarily for off-worlders, only to find more than twelve hundred separate warehousing companies with facilities spread out over a gigantic maze that was twice as large as all of New Marrakech.

With a sinking heart, he approached a fish-eyed gate-keeper at one of the many warehousing companies. The hive of storage cubicles and chambers seemed absolutely impenetrable. "Excuse me, sir, my father stored some things here and—"

"Serial number, level, and passcode please," the guard interrupted.

Ishaq shook his head and started again. "I don't have any of those things, but I thought if I gave you my father's name . . ."

The fish-eyed guard looked incredulously at him, then burst into a series of snorts, guffaws, and snuffles. "This will make an excellent Human joke," the guard said with another loud guffaw. "I can't wait to tell my friends."

Discouraged, Ishaq said, "I gather I said something humorous?"

"No warehouse on Fauldro ever uses *names*," the guard said in a tone that implied every intelligent being already knew this information. "That's why Fauldro is considered to have the safest storage in the Spiral Arm."

"No names," Ishaq repeated.

The guard shook his head. "Serial number, level, passcode."

Ishaq's shoulders sagged as he turned and headed for home. "Think of it as a challenge," he grumbled under his breath.

Straightening up, he forced himself to walk with confidence. By the time he returned to their living quarters on the *Ronin*, he had deduced that his father must have encoded the necessary data under another level of password and greater security. Now all he had to do was unlock the information.

He would start dinner and then get to work immediately.

— 13 —

At the flying academy, Akima continued to endure stupid "Human" insults, though few of the jokes even reached the level of being clever. She realized that the prejudice came from a misplaced fear. No other alien race understood why the powerful Drej had chosen Earth as their last target, so they dared not show compassion to Humans, lest their planet be marked next.

But as Akima went through her daily training exercises, listening to the instructors' teaching rather than their deprecating comments, she learned more than she had dreamed possible. Being a true pilot required talent, memory, skill, and imagination. With her reflexes and creativity, Akima outperformed most of the conservative stick-in-the-mud trainees in her class. Occasionally, as her scores got better, some of her fellow students even offered her words of grudging approval.

One morning the students gathered in the hangar bay and drew numbers for their assigned ships. The Fauldro

Flight Academy maintained a variety of vessels, and each trainee was required to know the systems on every machine. Some vessels were fast, others handled sluggishly. A few models had been discontinued because of hazardous design flaws.

Akima noticed that on the all-too-few occasions when they flew real ships, she drew the unsafe models far more often than any other student did; maybe the flight instructors were sending a message to the token Human in the class.

A supposedly random number came up beside her name, assigning her the piloting school's sole Sandor Gamma: a powerful, fast ship with tricky navigation systems and dangerously sluggish handling. Speed and clumsiness did not go together, and Sandor Gammas had been taken off the commercial market due to an unacceptably high number of crashes. But instead of complaining, Akima preferred to show them what the ship could do. At least they were actually flying today. She had to focus on the positive since the other trainees and the instructors were always searching for excuses to come down hard on her.

Beside her, Akima heard a noncommittal sound, a rumbling note that conveyed no excitement or disappointment. Her skilled but reserved classmate, Dhornan, stood tall, with angular limbs and moist skin that he misted repeatedly to keep his amphibious body damp. Colorful patches of symbiotic moss grew like fine feathers or thin, bright fur. Dhornan talked little, and his face was like a statue. Akima read no anger or friendliness there, no expression at all, but she knew he was competent and dedicated. He and Akima usually vied with each other for first place. Today, Akima intended to be better, though.

Dhornan had drawn the other fast ship in the school's retinue, a Condor Skimmer with double ion engines. Condors handled well through the thickest of nebulas; this one had even been flown directly across a comet's tail, earning its former pilot a spot on the school's wall of fame.

"Think you can beat me in that, Dhornan?" Akima nodded to the craft.

The ethereal alien made an ambiguous sound. None of the students on Fauldro even knew Dhornan's species, and the quiet alien didn't answer many questions.

Their instructor for the day, a hawk-billed old veteran named Herkimer Fhlax, shrieked out in his grating voice, "Attention, all of my talented students—" He turned black, beady eyes toward Akima. "And my Human student as well. Prepare to take your assigned ships. Today, the class will go sightseeing." He chirped and twittered, twitching his angular shoulders. "I will fly you through the Iron Canyons. You will follow me in formation . . ." He stepped back and raised his long beak as if to preen himself. "And I will try to lose you. Your job is to pace me at all times and return safely to the hangar."

"Sounds simple enough," Akima said to Dhornan. The tall alien looked vaguely around at the other students and did not answer.

"We shall see," Herkimer Fhlax said.

As she strapped on her helmet, the snide Gulcrecian student said to Akima, "We'll know soon enough if you're just a soil-sucker at heart, Human." Soil-sucker was a derogatory term that fliers used to describe planet-bound beings, comparing them to sluglike creatures of the same name that laboriously inched along the ground in the shadows and subsisted primarily on rotten vegetation.

Herkime Fhlax smirked at the comment. Then, with a jerky, bobbing gait, he trotted over to his own ship and climbed in, sealing the piloting hatch. He managed to prime his engines before the students realized their instructor meant to fly off, whether or not they were prepared to follow.

Akima scrambled toward her Sandor Gamma and jumped in, dismayed to see that the controls had been designed for a creature with a much larger body and three arms to manipulate buttons and levers. She didn't waste time grumbling, but punched up her engines and lifted the craft off the hangar floor while other students were still trying to find their vessels. Akima's sole focus was flight instructor Fhlax. He was the only one who mattered.

With silent, efficient movements, Dhornan sealed himself into his Condor Skimmer and ignited the double ion engines. Akima launched forward, getting a few seconds head start on the ethereal crack pilot. As other vessels streamed out of the hangar like a flock of startled birds, Akima pulled ahead, approaching the powerful craft flown by Herkimer Fhlax.

The flight instructor spun around, doing corkscrews in the air, showing off. Akima followed every one of his moves, feeling out the eccentricities and weak points in the controls of her Sandor Gamma. The message had been drilled into her over and over again: *Know your ship.* She had to understand how fast she could push the engines, how tightly the skyrudders could maintain control.

In Fauldro's atmosphere, winds and weather made a substantial difference. Out in the vacuum and weightlessness of space, flight was a different experience. Akima promised herself she would learn it all.

Akima knew she was not just some simulator jockey. She had studied hard, she had training and practice, and she'd logged quite a few flight hours—even if most of them were in a cargo hauler. But she was ready for this. She was no soil-sucker, not planet-bound, not imprisoned by bars of gravity. Rarely in her life had she felt the need to show others that she was better than they were, but when her abilities were questioned she met the challenge head-on. Right now, she had something to prove.

Fhlax roared upward at full speed into a thick cloud bank, and Akima switched on her tracker, using sensors to detect the metal of his hull, familiarizing herself with the scan signature of the instructor's craft. When he plunged into the gauzy thunderhead, she was able to follow, but several other trainee ships were left behind, lost.

Akima followed the instructor through the gray soup, dodging crackles of lightning until Fhlax burst through the top of the island in the sky. He soared southward with Akima close on his tail, Dhornan not far behind, and only a dozen of the twenty students still in formation.

Above the cloud banks, the sun was dazzling. Akima had to dim the canopy windows to protect her eyes. Some of the other aliens from dim worlds would have even more trouble than she did.

Fhlax descended toward thick, purple fan-forests, skimmed along the fleecy treetops, and did his best to lose the following ships. But Akima maintained her sensor lock and had no trouble keeping up. He flew up, over a line of gray, lumpy mountains that looked like weathered molars thrust up from blackened ground.

Several students had dropped out of the chase through sheer lack of speed, their vessels unable to sustain the pursuit. Though Akima's hot-rod vessel wasn't the safest of the group, at least she could keep up.

Now, a webwork of deep cracks lay spread before them, black lightning bolts burned into the ground. The deep chasms were surrounded by rugged rocks, and steam rose up from the jagged gorges. These were the Iron Canyons, channels fed by volcanic springs, emitting clouds of sulfurous steam that provided an isolated yet fertile ecosystem.

Thick feather forests and sporetrees populated the canyon floors, a wilderness so dense and lush that few explorers could penetrate its depths. Herkimer Fhlax led them straight toward the primary gorge. "Where do you think you can run now?" Akima muttered.

The instructor's ship tilted downward in a steep descent, and Akima followed in the backwash of his thrusters.

Fhlax plunged between the walls of the canyon where the main fissure spread out into many fingers. The side gorges held a primeval forest of tall, gray-green trees. The towering growths had feathery branches and rounded balls filled with ripe spores.

Did the instructor mean to land down there? Or try to hide in the forest? Akima couldn't see how that was possible. She could barely see through the yellow-gray brimstone smoke and steam.

Not far behind, to the rear of her left wing, Dhornan's

Condor Skimmer paced her. His double ion engines could have overtaken her vessel, but Dhornan seemed in no hurry. Fhlax's instructions had not been for anyone to be *first* at following him, just to follow him successfully. Akima wished she had the amphibious alien's cool confidence.

She was looking behind her, not paying attention to her primary target—the only real target—when Herkimer Fhlax ducked to the treeline and increased the thrust of his engines, skimming directly over the canopy. His engine backwash rippled the trees and churned them into a chaos of thrashing branches, burst nodules, and flying spores—like a surge of whitewater rapids.

The feather trees released swarms of delicate, puffy seeds. Great clusters of ivory-white spores exploded into clouds. Akima gasped, as if a blizzard had suddenly materialized around her. The grainy spores flew high, swirled up in currents by the passage of Fhlax's ship. She couldn't see! Despite her instinctive need to withdraw, to pull up to safety, she knew this was exactly what Fhlax wanted her to do.

Instead, Akima fixed her attention on her instruments, relying on scanners to display a safe path. Her every reflex screamed against flying blindly through the clouds of spores and puffy seeds, but she watched the blip of Fhlax's ship. She followed closely, matching him move for move, though he couldn't see her either. Akima dreaded flying close to sheer and unexpected canyon walls, but if she followed the instructor, at least he would splatter into the rock before she did. Maybe, just maybe, she'd have time to pull up.

Behind her, Dhornan's ship plunged through the spore-cloud as well, invisible in the swirling seed storm.

Rapidly, though, his powerful ion engines—designed for use in open space with no resistance—became choked with seeds. With strangled engine intakes, Dhornan's ship wavered and chugged, trying to keep up, but he soon fell back.

Akima hoped the silent, self-absorbed student didn't crash and become lost inside the wilderness of the Iron Canyons. No doubt the piloting school would send in rescue teams to save his life . . . but Akima couldn't imagine anything more embarrassing.

On the scanner, instructor Fhlax took a sharp turn to port, streaking down one of the side canyons. Akima followed, banking sharply to the left as a rugged gray wall towered in front of her like a giant hand that meant to swat her out of the skies. But she did a roll, and to her surprise, the Sandor Gamma responded exceptionally, as if all it had wanted in its design life was a pilot who would trust the ship to perform up to par.

The seed storm faded before long and they cruised to the edges of the tributary canyons. Herkimer Fhlax gave up on the game at last and circled back, taking a circuitous return route to the Flight Academy. Only Akima's ship had made it all the way through the obstacle course. . . .

When they arrived back at the hangar and landed their ships, Fhlax seemed both annoyed and unsettled that Akima had won this round of testing sessions. Over the next few hours, trainees drifted back in their own vessels. Some had returned a long time before, others had simply gotten lost and transmitted requests for homing beacons so they could make their way back.

Herkimer Fhlax clacked his hawklike bill, but was honor bound to state the obvious. "Akima wins the competition today." He made a squeaking sound as if it pained him to utter the words. "She holds the title of Best in Class—until someone else beats her. I trust that won't take long."

Then the instructor went to the administrative offices where he arranged a search and rescue party for Dhornan.

– 14 –

That evening, the instructors assembled inside the debriefing room, sitting in panel formation to give their general remarks first before meeting with each student individually. In front of them stood head instructor Herkimer Fhlax alongside an alien Akima had never seen before.

His equine face had a peachy complexion that darkened into tan on the rest of his body. Long, floppy ears hung down on either side of his head, which made his bulbous eyes seem to bulge out even further than they did. The long torso and ears were counterbalanced by incongruously short, stubby arms and legs.

The instructor spoke, raising his hatchet face like a proud eagle. "One of the advantages of attending Fauldro's Flight Academy is the wide variety of opportunities that will open up for you. Today, I am pleased to present to you Mr. Glk, a representative of one of the most generous employers in the Spiral Arm. Many of our finest pilots have been placed with his organization. Glk, I believe you have a few words to say?"

"Mmm, mmm, yes." Glk bounced up and down on his stubby legs, almost lost his balance, frantically wheeled his little arms, regained his balance, and said, "Yes," again. "Each season my employer authorizes me . . . mmm, yes, mmm . . . to recruit five of the most talented pilots from each class. This offer is extended only to the most promising students. In our employ, even the best of you will find sufficient challenges for your skills, and if you succeed, the rewards are even greater than the challenges. Mmm, yes."

Forefinger tapping against her lips, Akima began to listen with real interest. She was the top student in her class, so she had no doubt that she was one of the "chosen few" to whom Glk would extend this job offer. Unless the mere fact that she was a Human would disqualify her.

"Do you have any questions so far, mmm?" Glk asked. His floppy ears pricked up.

Dhornan spoke, his voice toneless. "What kind of work is this, and how dangerous?"

"Danger, mmm, yes," Glk said. He loudly blew air through his flexible lips, like a horse snorting. "We have business concerns in every area of the Spiral Arm, and since the recent reappearance of the terrible Drej"—he shuddered and blinked his bulbous eyes—"there are risks associated with even routine trade flights. Thus, more than ever before, we have a need for the best pilots."

Glk pointed to a diagram of the settled region of the galaxy. "Occasionally our pilots are required to break through military blockades, make deliveries to troubled territories, or outrun Drej Stingers." He shuddered again. "Since there seems to be no predicting where and why the Drej ships will attack, Mr. Golbus prefers to hire only the most capable pilots."

Akima's heart skipped a beat. "Would that be Golbus of Solbrecht?" *The crime lord?* Her hope for earning top credits in a job straight out of the academy faded. Even the prospect of flying against Drej, which she had found intriguing, could not outweigh what she knew about Golbus.

Glk's bulbous eyes blinked and narrowed slightly. "Mmm, Solbrecht . . . Regional Headquarters, yes."

"That'll be enough questions, Human," Herkimer Fhlax snapped.

She saw Dhornan regarding her coolly, but could read no emotion on his alien face.

Fhlax tapped his long teaching staff on the tabletop with a whiplike cracking sound. "After your debriefing, the following students are invited to meet with the recruiter for Mr. Golbus. Based entirely on your scores in simulation and actual flying."

When he read off the names, Akima's was at the top of the list. But she hastily scribbled a note firmly turning down the offer of employment. She handed the note to Glk before walking out. Akima had no intention of ever dealing with Golbus again.

Glk bounced up and down on his squat legs as he waited for his interstellar connection to go through. The toll charges spun upward with dizzying speed.

Finally, Golbus's impatient face appeared on the communications screen. His amber eyes narrowed, and the fingers of all four hands drummed a steady tattoo on his desk. "Yes, what is it?" he said gruffly, then looked down at the collect charges clicking along the side of his screen. "And talk fast!"

"Mmm, yes, it's Glk," the recruiter said unnecessarily. Golbus gave him a withering look, and Glk's long ears drooped. "Yes, success to report. Mmm, four pilots recruited. I, mmm, believe they will perform remarkably well on even the most difficult of your smuggling routes."

"Are they the top four?" Golbus asked sharply.

"Top? Mmm, no," Glk admitted. "The best student, a Human . . . she declined our offer. From a comment she made, I believe she, mmm, had heard of you before?"

"A Human!" Golbus roared, raising his upper hands as if ready to strangle someone. "I never authorized you to extend our offer to any Humans. The Drej would target us for sure."

"Humans, mmm, no. You never mentioned Humans," Glk said. "But you gave me the strictest of instructions, mmm? Recruit only the top pilots, you said, sir. Mmm, she was number one in her class."

"But you know how I feel about Humans," Golbus said. "And the Drej!" Then an uncharacteristic look of true horror crossed Golbus's face. "Tell me that Fauldro hasn't been overrun by Humans. If the Drej ever got wind of it, they could do some real damage. They could mark the whole world for their revenge—and I have too much at stake in the banks and storage vaults to let that happen."

"Mmm, no, not many Humans," Glk assured him. "Chancellor Jaxor tells me that she is one of perhaps eight on the planet at this time."

"So this upstart Human girl came to Fauldro alone?"

Golbus pressed. "And how does she know about me? I try to keep my name out of public view."

"Mmm, no. Not alone. I found out what I could about her. Mmm, I was going to go to her later. While the other students live in barracks at the Flight Academy, the Human lives with a Mantrin weapons specialist and a Human boy on board their ship." His ears pricked up. "They came here from Solbrecht—perhaps that is where they heard of you, Lord Golbus, mmm?"

"What?" Golbus shouted.

Glk stammered, then blew a long stream of air through his flexible lips. "Of course I will not go there to offer her the position, now that you have made it clear that—"

Golbus cut him off with chopping motions of both right hands. "No, I meant what did you say about a Mantrin? A weapons specialist?"

Glk swallowed hard, realizing that the crime lord was angry at him but not understanding why. "Mmm, a female, I believe. And the Human male is still young, in the larval stage, I believe." He tapped his fingers together, stalling for time. "Yes, that's correct. Female Mantrin, female Human, male Human. All together, and they came here—in a very fine, new ship, I might add—from Solbrecht." Finally, he had an idea. "Are they, mmm, business associates of yours, Lord Golbus?"

The crime lord stopped drumming his fingers on the desk as a wave of fury passed over him, then astonishingly faded as he brought his anger under control. He folded his four hands across his chest and nodded curtly as a devious expression crossed his gaunt, grayish face. "Congratulations, Glk. You've actually been most helpful."

Glk shifted his weight from one stubby leg to the other, hoping that his boss was not merely lulling him into a false sense of security so that he could punish him later. Golbus was famous for his convoluted punishments.

"I have a new assignment for you," Golbus went on. "I want you to keep an eye on that Human girl *and* her two friends. Especially the Mantrin. Watch every move they make. Can you do that?"

Glk nodded his equine head. "For how long?"

Golbus's eyes grew hard as titanium. "Until I arrive. Suddenly, I find I have urgent business on Fauldro . . . and a score to settle. I'll be coming there to oversee the situation personally." With that, he cut off the connection.

As the screen went blank, every tensed muscle in Glk's body went limp, and he sank to the floor in a relieved heap. He hoped Golbus wouldn't notice how outrageously high the communications charge had run.

The key to Mohammed's holoscroll still haunted Ishaq. He had already cracked the first code, which had led them here to Fauldro, one planet among millions. And here there were millions of storage containers in the sprawling warehouse district that covered a large part of the continent. Without specific information, Ishaq was just as lost now as he had been at the very beginning.

Based on his success with Mozart in the first place, he tried the names of composers and artists and writers who had been his father's favorites. He tried names of relatives, languages, games they had played together.

Before Ishaq had left the used-weapons shop that afternoon, Stith had told him, "You're workin' at this too hard, kid. Akima tells me your father was a smart guy, so he must have used a password that only his trusted friends could figure out. Go back to the basics. Think about exactly what he gave you, and what you know about him."

Taking the advice to heart, Ishaq had started again from scratch with the holoscroll laid out in front of him. "Start with what my father gave me," he murmured.

Mohammed had rushed into their doomed home on New Marrakech to retrieve this holoscroll because it was so important. Important enough to die for. *But that wasn't the only thing!* Ishaq picked up the tiny sculpture of Buddha his father had also been grasping when they'd found him in the collapsed, burning home.

Maybe these two things were meant to work together in some way.

Following that line of reasoning, Ishaq had already scrutinized the tiny sculpture to see if it contained a key of some sort, then used a high-resolution scanner on board the *Ronin*, but the scan had turned up nothing. Now he held the objects side by side in front of him, as if by staring at them he could *will* the solution into existence.

He sighed again. "You're workin' too hard, kid," he reminded himself. "Back to the basics."

Letting his eyes fall shut, he tried to empty his mind of all conscious thought. Slowly, he opened a chink in his mind and let memories of his father seep back in. Washing their hands in the trickling fountains before going to prayer in the spaceship mosque at the center of New Marrakech, cooking meals together, listening to music . . . Mozart had been his father's favorite, a bond that he had shared with Ishaq's mother—so much so that

Ishaq's mother had named the family cat Figaro. Ishaq's mother had died a year before the Drej attack. Their cat, a fluffy gray Persian, had escaped from Earth with Mohammed and Ishaq.

A smile touched the corners of the young man's mouth. He had only been eight when Figaro died, but he still remembered. Something made a connection in Ishaq's mind, and he hummed the sprightly overture to Mozart's *Marriage of Figaro*.

Strangely, the Buddha statuette began to vibrate in his hand. He opened one eye to look at it, but continued humming. Then Ishaq's eyes widened.

The sculpture pulsed and gave off a faint luminescence. Still humming, he moved the tiny Buddha above the holoscroll, then below it, then to the left, right, top, and bottom, but to no effect.

He stopped humming. The statuette ceased its vibrations. Next, Ishaq hummed a few notes from the second movement of *Eine Kleine Nachtmusik*. Nothing. Mozart's Symphony Number 29 also produced no reaction. Ishaq began again with the overture to *Marriage of Figaro*. The vibrations resumed.

He stood the tiny Buddha on the input pad of the holoscroll and found that the base was a perfect fit. A moment later, a cascade of information flowed from the holoscroll: lists, names, dates, items, serial number, level, passcode. The location of the storage vault in the labyrinth of the Fauldro warehouse district!

Everything Ishaq had hoped for was there, and far, far more.

—15—

Akima and Stith met at the spaceport and arrived back at the *Ronin*, where Ishaq greeted them at the door hatch. So deep was she in her concerns about Golbus and his "recruiter" that she hardly noticed the excitement on the boy's face. "Akima, I have news!"

"So do I," she said.

"Yeah, me too," Stith said.

"My news is good," Ishaq ventured.

"Mine's bad," Akima said.

"Mine could go either way," Stith said. "We just got word at the shop that a very influential buyer is coming to Fauldro within the next few days, ready to make some serious deals. Everyone with any kind of merchandise is gearing up for big sales. Real competitive. Like I said, could be good, could be bad." She looked at Akima. "Now you."

With one hand Akima rubbed the back of her neck below her black hair. "A recruiter came to the academy today, promising heaps of credits to any top student who would sign on with his employer."

"But what's wrong with that?" Ishaq asked.

Akima gritted her teeth. "His employer was Golbus."

Stith growled, planting her fists on her hips. "Nobody forced you to accept the offer, did they?"

Akima shook her head. "I declined, but I'm afraid that some of my talented classmates accepted. They don't know what they're getting into—and I can't believe Chancellor Jaxor would let a slimeball like Golbus recruit here." She sighed and turned her almond-shaped eyes toward Ishaq. With one hand, she flicked a few dyed-purple strands out of her eyes. "Okay, I'm ready for some good news."

Ishaq's green eyes glowed with feverish excitement. "I broke the code!" Akima nodded distractedly. Ishaq took Akima's shoulders and forced her to look into his eyes. "I broke my father's code. We know where the storage unit is."

Stith gave a loud squawk of delight, sprang up on her powerful legs and slapped the ceiling with one palm, then landed again with a muffled thud. "You did it, kid! You've been working on that for ages."

All thoughts of Golbus were swept from Akima's mind. "Code? You mean we can go there and see . . . everything?"

"Everything," Ishaq said in a voice that held no uncertainty. "Are you two going to just stand here like a couple of soil-suckers, or are you coming with me to find it?"

Stith grabbed Akima by the arm and propelled her into motion. "We're with you, kid. Lead on."

• • •

The storage district, regardless of time of day, was a hive of activity. As daylight shaded into evening colors, Ishaq talked nonstop all the way to the warehouse company named in the holoscroll. Infected by his enthusiasm, Stith and Akima peppered him with questions whenever he paused.

"The system here is ingenious," Ishaq explained. "Absolute anonymity for whoever rents a storage chamber, for whatever reason. Aliens from one end of the Spiral Arm to the other can stash their valuables: heirlooms, financial records, investment relics waiting to get old enough to be worth something, even blood and DNA samples from family members, preserved as a family tree. With all of Fauldro's guarantees and interlocks, there's no way anyone could have traced the contents to my father, or even to Earth. Occasionally, someone will mark their storage chamber from the outside, but according to my father's notes, he purposely left no markings. It looks just like a million others."

They approached the burly reptilian guard at the gate of the storage company Mohammed had chosen. The guard eyed the two Humans suspiciously. "Serial number, level, passcode," he intoned. Behind him, structures and alleys and streets were filled with squarish containers, some the size of buildings, some small booths. But no one could even enter the section of the sprawling warehouse city without access privileges.

Nervous that something might still go wrong, Ishaq gave the required information in a shaky voice. The reptilian guard grunted and seemed to lose all interest in them. "Take one of the courtesy scooters inside, and you can fly to your unit. It'll take about an hour from here."

He dropped the first layer of the triple-stage security barrier to allow them through, raised the barrier again, and cycled them through the next two layers. A scutbot topped by blinking lights met them on the other side to lead them to their storage area.

Akima slapped Ishaq on the back as they climbed aboard one of the clunky hoverscooters. "It worked!"

"So far, so good," Stith agreed. "Follow that scutbot."

Akima powered up the hoverscooter and raced after the blinking device. They flew along for kilometers between stacks of massive storage containers, weaving their way around honeycombs of smaller units.

The storage area sprawled off to the horizon, and Akima realized why Ishaq had had so much trouble locating one simple unit. "I guess you don't bump into our little cubicle by accident," she said.

Stith growled. "I don't bump into anything by accident."

As Ishaq had predicted, most of the vaults were entirely featureless and unmarked, but one of the rusty rooftops below them bore a symbol of a sword through a ring of barbed wire, or perhaps it was thorns.

"Anybody know what that means?" Akima asked.

"I think it's the mark of some religious order," Stith said. "That triangle design over there"—she pointed to a rundown-looking chamber—"means it's another Hodrian storage box. You'll see plenty of them."

The skies had turned full dark overhead, and pinkish yellow lights blazed down around all of the storage containers by the time the scutbot finally led them to their destination, a big, unmarked chamber the size of a house. "I guess this is it," Akima said.

Ishaq, full of awe, went forward as the scutbot hovered in front of the door. The blinking contraption extended a hexagonal probe from its underbelly and plugged it into the keyslot at the bottom of the ten-meter-high bay doors. The scutbot projected a holographic keypad into the air above it and blinked a message in several languages. "Confirm serial number and passcode."

With unsteady fingers, Ishaq entered the information on the holographic keypad. For a few seconds, nothing happened. Akima took his hand and gave it a squeeze. Stith draped a muscular arm around his shoulder. Then, with a faint, rumbling groan, the bay doors split in the middle and slid aside. Brilliant lighting flooded the cavernous chamber.

The scutbot blinked several times, spat the hexagonal key into Ishaq's palm, then rushed off into the night. Ishaq watched it go. "I hope I can remember the way back."

"Didn't see any skeletons lying around on our way here," Akima observed.

Staring in amazement, Ishaq seemed afraid to enter this place he had waited so long to see. Heaving an impatient sigh, Stith pushed both Humans through the doorway, then stepped inside. The massive doors shut behind them.

Earth's greatest cultural treasure house.

Standing just inside the vault, Ishaq found himself hardly able to breathe. Each objet d'art was preserved in an individual microstasis field to protect it from environmental effects and jostling.

In a hushed, reverent voice, Ishaq began to speak. "My father's notes said that in the last days of Earth, during the chaos of evacuation while the space military tried to hold off the Drej mothership, his Titan team rounded up all the cultural treasures they could. They gathered art from the Louvre, the Vatican, great museums, and even private collections." They walked slowly up an aisle of drawings, sculptures, paintings. "I never thought I'd get to see it all."

Stith grunted appreciatively at statues, watercolors, ancient tapestries. "Huh, and they say Humans have no culture." Ishaq and Akima both shot her a sharp look, and she protested, "Hey, I never said *I* believed that. Sheesh, touchy!"

They roamed for hours through the amazing archives, stopping to play snippets of music, looking at holographic video sequences that portrayed dance or religious ceremonies. They scrolled through electronic repositories of literature and poetry, photography, cinematography, and holography.

They viewed samples of architecture, ceramics, blown glass, jewelry, metalwork, and religious artifacts until their minds could absorb no more. Here before them lay the very best of humanity's achievements, waiting to be redistributed as soon as mankind had a new home.

"This is what my grandmother wanted me to understand each time she showed me a trinket from Earth and told me a story about it. Humans have a richer past, more creativity and accomplishment, than I could ever have known if I hadn't seen this. I feel like I'm standing inside Grandmother's collection—only a million times more fantastic."

"My father sacrificed his life so that we wouldn't lose this," Ishaq said. "Humanity, I mean. We . . ." His throat tightened with emotion and he could not finish his sentence. He looked at Akima and saw that she was moved, too. Tears ran unchecked from her warm brown eyes.

She hugged him. "You know, Ishaq, up until now I've always doubted all the talk about working together and building a central place for all Humans to call home. But now that I see this, I think somehow—someday— we're going to make it happen."

Stith threw her muscular arms around both Humans. "And if there's any way I can help, you can count on me."

Glk entered the storage district, following orders. Golbus had merchandise stashed with almost every warehouse company on Fauldro, so the sneaky recruiter had all the information he needed. It had been a simple enough matter to bribe the guard to look the other way when Glk did not follow the scutbot usher, but instead followed the Humans and the Mantrin from a distance, keeping well out of sight and in the shadows.

Golbus would be very interested to know what the Humans were hiding.

—16—

The warehouse district on Fauldro was a beautiful sight to see, stretching out for kilometer upon kilometer. On the observation balcony of his tall administrative tower, Jaxor, the chancellor of the Flight Academy waited alongside one of the heavy investors in the storage business. Both gazed across the vista of armored containers, each one arranged and catalogued according to a confidential system developed over the centuries by the bureaucrats of Fauldro. It stretched all the way to the misty horizon.

Watching from the high balcony, Jaxor wanted to weep for each container he was losing moment by moment. He watched the heavy contract haulers come down from the skies like an invading army. Jaxor had no choice but to let the pilots locate the requested containers, then seize the storage units with powerful tractor beams. *Another one gone!* Clumsy cargo haulers ripped each container out of the matrix, dragging them up through deep-blue skies streaked with vermilion clouds.

With each lost container, each diminished asset, Jaxor felt as if they were pulling his teeth, perhaps even ripping his organs out.

"But how can you do this?" His voice was high-pitched with rage and despair. He turned to the leader of the Rutan Conglomeration, a creature with broad shoulders, a sharp black horn where his nose should have been, and nostrils where most species kept their ears. "I assure you that our facilities are completely secure," Jaxor insisted. "All records are confidential. You have nothing to worry about."

The Rutani turned his blockish head toward Jaxor so sharply that it looked as if the black horn might rip the air. "And what will you do when the Drej learn there are Humans here on Fauldro? They are back, you know. Only a few months ago they attacked the Human Drifter colony of New Marrakech."

"But who cares about a Drifter colony?" Jaxor said. "I heard some rumors, yes, but what does that matter? New Marrakech is far from here."

"Not far enough." The Rutani looked out across the skyline as cargo haulers continued to uproot expensive, armored storage units and carry them into space toward another secret archive facility. The Rutani would never tell Jaxor which world had outbid Fauldro.

"Remember what the Drej did to Earth—and before that, Qu'ut Prime. What will you do if they come *here*, Chancellor Jaxor? You have no defenses." He snorted loudly, a fluting sound forced through his hollow horn, echoed by the nostrils at the sides of his head. "The Rutan Conglomeration's biological specimens and genealogical records are too valuable to risk on your over-confident assurances."

Jaxor swallowed against a suddenly dry throat. Fauldro and its famous storage areas could survive without the business from the Conglomeration . . . but this was only the start. His meeting schedule for the day was already filled with other commercial representatives, longtime customers. With genuine dread he knew that this incident was merely the first in what was sure to be an unpleasant avalanche.

Deep in his throat, Jaxor made a strangled sound, knowing he could do nothing to force the Rutani to keep their storage units here. "But what if we get rid of all the Humans? Evict them from the planet?" he said, still trying. "We could remove all trace of their contamination. There are far fewer Humans than there are cargo containers from the Rutan Conglomeration."

"That would be a good start," the alien said, then the nostrils at the sides of his head contracted, as if to avoid an unpleasant odor. "Unfortunately, too late. We need to ensure safety right now." The creature bent its squarish head until its sharp black horn could have stabbed Jaxor in the neck. "However, because of our long-term relationship with the fine government on Fauldro, we will reconsider our position once you have . . . removed any possibility of threat. Solve the Human problem, Chancellor Jaxor, and the Rutani may be amenable to doing business with you again."

Then, the conversation clearly over, the Rutani businessman turned and watched with an expression of apparent pleasure as the groups of heavy haulers continued to lift cargo units. Tractor beams shimmered in the air, carrying massive containers, one after another, out to space. Each loss left a hole like an open grave in the beautiful storage matrix that had brought Fauldro so much fame and success.

Stith always found reasons to grumble. It was one of her talents, along with knowing the ins and outs of practically every weapons system ever designed. Here on Fauldro, which supposedly stored everything for any race in the galaxy, a melting pot of pieces that never actually melted, she had spent all morning trudging from market cubicle to business establishment in search of ammo packs for her favorite, portable high-yield blasters.

Back on Solbrecht, Golbus's henchmen had unwittingly provided her with the weapons when they refurbished and restocked the *Ronin*. Stith enjoyed using the blasters, loved the feel of vibration in her hands, the warm smell of ionized air, the crackle of beautiful, bright colors as the beams lanced out to blow up anything they touched.

Unfortunately, though, such portable high-yield blasters were illegal in most systems, which meant that finding ammo packs could be difficult.

She grumbled again, clacking her hard mouth nibs together as she stomped through the alleyways toward the main market center. Stith supposed she could find a service specialist, an "item locator," who would charge a huge commission, but would guarantee finding any object she desired.

Stith hadn't exhausted her own resources yet. And she wasn't through grumbling.

As she stalked toward the main commerce hub on the outskirts of the storage district, Stith heard the hubbub of a crowd, squeaks and snorts and whistles in countless alien languages. The streets grew crowded as more spectators pressed toward this gathering or rally, or whatever it was. Stith hated it when other creatures got in the way, but luckily her elbows were sharp and hard.

She strode forward, tail lashing from side to side, arms in front of her, ready to shoulder her way through insensitive crowds. "Whoa! Make room, make room!" She knocked some creatures aside, but took minimal satisfaction from it; grumbling was actually more entertaining.

In the front of the square, standing tall on a large podium, was Chancellor Jaxor, who had complained so loudly about letting Akima into the Flight Academy. Stith knew that such powerful men didn't have their fingers in only one pie; she suspected that with the lucrative storage business on Fauldro, Jaxor probably controlled other commercial establishments as well.

Now Jaxor raised his voice and railed at the gathered population. Citizens of Fauldro normally minded their own business because almost all businesses here *depended on* privacy. On this planet, any creature could store any object and be completely confident that no one else would learn a storage unit's location or contents.

In front of the crowd, Jaxor's passionate words boomed out of speakers that had been mounted around the square. Stith grumbled again. So, the chancellor had been planning this little spectacle for some time. It obviously wasn't an impromptu rally.

"The Drej have returned!" Jaxor shouted, and his listeners stirred, peering nervously up at the skies. "No one knows why they pick their targets, but we do know who they are. Some species, like *Humans,* have foolishly intimidated the Drej enough for them to strike back. So far they have left most of us alone—but not *Humans*." Jaxor paused while a loud sneer and groan rippled through the crowd.

The immediate reaction disturbed Stith, and she realized that the chancellor had planted accomplices among the spectators just to rile up the crowd. "Dirty trick," she muttered.

"We know that the Humans must have done something, committed some crime to warrant the ultimate punishment of the Drej. There can be no question about it. Why else would the Drej destroy Earth?"

"Nobody knows!" somebody shouted from the crowd.

"It's because the Humans are a threat—and therefore a threat to us all," Jaxor answered. "And now the Drej are sniffing around again. Scout ships have been seen in numerous systems." He waited again as a murmur of dismay and fear rippled through the crowd. Stith's tail lashed back and forth. She wanted to pull Jaxor's ears off, one at a time, and then start on other appendages.

"The Drej attacked a Human Drifter colony, and they will continue hunting down any survivors. They will seek out Humans—" He paused and then bellowed in a louder, ominous tone, "—and anyone who associates with Humans. We on Fauldro must protect ourselves."

"So get rid of the Humans!" someone shouted from the crowd, presumably one of Jaxor's shills. "We don't need them on Fauldro."

"Fortunately, we don't have many of them here," Chancellor Jaxor said, sounding reasonable now. "It won't take much of an effort to remove them if we work together. Fauldro must guarantee safety for its investors, all those who store their valuables with us. But how can we possibly do this while we have . . ." he paused to sneer the word again, "*Humans* among us?"

Stith did not like where this speech was going. Not at all. "Hey! You don't know what the Drej want." She raised her voice, but not far enough to be heard above the noisy crowd. "I don't need anybody to tell me who to hate. You're just picking on Humans because they're an easy target."

Several members of the crowd glared at her as if they wanted to yank Stith's tail out by its roots. She would have been happy for them to try.

Jaxor lifted a plaque in his hands. "I have here the coordinates of a ship owned by Humans parked in our own docks. Is this reckless Human pilot putting our entire planet at risk? I, for one, am not willing to take that chance."

"Destroy the ship!" someone yelled. "Get the Humans off Fauldro!"

Indignant, Stith rose higher on her enormous legs. "You can't divulge the locations of specific ships," she bellowed, wanting to be heard this time. "That goes against your confidentiality agreement."

"It's a matter of security when it's a *Human* ship," snapped a scaly faced alien.

Another person added in a smaller voice, "Well, it is in the standard agreement. Divulging such—"

"What are you two? Human lovers?" someone shouted.

Stith snarled, "If you let Jaxor give away that location, what's to stop him from doing the same to all of you, whenever he finds some excuse to—"

Before she could finish, though, Jaxor bellowed out the landing bay number where the *Ronin* was docked.

Fiery with anger, the crowd turned about. Jaxor continued to shout, but the gathered aliens had already made up their minds. The chancellor now did his best to direct the mob where he wanted them to go.

Seeing she could do little against so many angry creatures, Stith galloped off, covering a great deal of distance on her long powerful legs. She had to warn Akima and Ishaq before the mob came after them.

– 17 –

Thanks to Stith's great strides, she came bounding back to Akima's ship well ahead of the mob. Even so, she could hear the shouting, chanting, and angry growls not far behind.

"Hey, wake up!" she shouted into the open hatch. "We don't have much time to put up barricades."

Ishaq, busy going over his preliminary catalog of the items he had found in the cultural storage unit, blinked his wide green eyes. "Barricades?" He poked his head out of the *Ronin*'s hatch. "To protect us from what?"

"Them!" From the upper deck, Akima pointed down the narrow alleys leading to the landing field. The forerunners of an angry crowd came around the corner of a tall hangar building.

They scrambled on a variety of feet, flexible legs, flippers, and tentacles. Many brandished makeshift weapons, items that had never been meant for causing destruction. Some mob members seemed ready to rip into the hull plates using nothing more than sucker-tipped fingers or sharpened claws.

Ishaq's eyes widened further. "Stith! What did you say to rile them up?"

The weapons specialist thrashed her muscular tail as she stomped up the ramp into the *Ronin*, and Ishaq had to leap back out of the way. "Wasn't me. Chancellor Jaxor's got them all primed for a little Human hunt." She slammed and sealed the hatch, then clambered up to their storage chambers. She began hauling out the boxes and crates of weapons they had tricked Golbus's henchmen into providing.

Stith took out a portable high-yield blaster. "Now this baby would take care of the whole mob." But she tossed it aside with a loud clatter. "Unfortunately, I couldn't find any ammo packs out in the market." Instead, Stith grabbed lasers, concussion grenades, shrapnel mines.

As Akima surveyed the firepower, she said firmly, "You're not just going to kill them all."

"I *could*." Stith hefted an ominous-looking weapon with several nozzles, beam focusers, and an array of controls marked in a language Akima didn't recognize. "Ah, but that would only help us out in the short term. Afterward, the Fauldro military'd declare us criminals and take us down."

Akima could hear shouts and yells from outside, coming closer. A loud bang resounded like a gunshot: a cobblestone thrown against the hull of their ship.

"On the other hand," Stith said, "might have no choice but to settle for a short-term solution."

Ishaq had climbed up to a high viewport that led out to an observation platform. "I see Chancellor Jaxor, but he's at the rear of the mob, just directing them. He doesn't seem to be doing anything himself."

"Figures," Akima said. Stith looked down at her extensive array of weapons, silently thanking Golbus for his unwitting generosity.

More thumps vibrated through the hull.

"How can we take off with so many of them out there?" Ishaq shouted.

"One sonic detonator would improve our odds," Stith said. "By quite a bit."

"And turn them all to jelly," Akima said. "That's not my first choice."

"Then give me a Plan B," Stith said.

Akima tapped her lower lip and brushed a strand of purple hair out of her eyes. She ran to the wall to check the *Ronin*'s complement of safety provisions and smiled with relief. "Looks like Ringus the Refurbisher took care of everything."

A thunderous drumbeat pounded against the hull, a rhythmic succession of hammering sounds as the rioters pressed against the vessel. "Right this way. Follow me for Plan B," Akima said.

They raced to the upper cargo deck, high above the crowd. When Akima opened the hatches to stand exposed in the air, the angry aliens went wild, roaring for Human blood.

Stith leaned over the edge of the platform, her legs coiled and tense, her clawed hands clenching the rail. Her mouth nibs clacked together, and she flashed a glance at the two Humans. "Come on, Akima—just one little concussion grenade? It'll get their attention."

Akima took a step to the edge of the observation platform, and the mob shrieked even louder. Jaxor pointed furiously at them. Some aliens hurled objects higher, but no one could reach the upper cargo hatch.

"Looks like I've already got their attention," Akima said.

"Death to Humans!" someone shouted.

"Don't bring the Drej here. Keep us safe!" an alien voice squawked.

"Humans, go home!" cried one particularly dimwitted creature. Akima wanted to remind him that Humans no longer *had* a home, but decided she could outrage them in a more effective way.

"Hey, it's gonna be tough for us to *leave* if you damage our ship," she yelled down.

The crowd simmered, quieting a little, then they roared louder from the rear. Jaxor screamed, "You had no right to land here in the first place. Fauldro doesn't want you, not in the Flight Academy, not anywhere on our planet."

The aliens screamed and cheered. Ironically, few of them were original natives of Fauldro either.

Stith unshouldered the two largest, meanest energy weapons she had carried from the stockpile and held them out in a threatening gesture. The crowd drew back, still yelling but intimidated now.

Jaxor egged them on from his safe position far to the rear. "Go forward! They can't kill us all! You'll be martyrs to save our beloved Fauldro."

"All right—gave 'em a chance to be reasonable," Stith said, looking at Ishaq and Akima. "Didn't we? You both saw it."

"Right," Akima said. "Now we use Plan B." She dragged out one of the emergency fire-suppression hoses and gestured for Stith and Ishaq to do the same. Together, the three of them pulled heavy tubes from beside the cargo hatch. Akima flicked the activation switch.

Gouts of thick, grayish-white foam spewed out onto the crowds, raining in all directions. The goop fell in heavy clots, coating the nearest aliens with a smothering froth. Balanced on her muscular hind legs, Stith raised her nozzle high, spraying the gelatinous, fire-retardant foam in a beautiful parabolic arc, down upon the shrieking mob. With disappointment, she saw that her stream did not reach all the way to where Jaxor stood.

Soon, the whole unruly crowd was coated like a living mass of dessert. They tried to fling the clinging, fluffy substance from uniforms, headscales, and nose-slits. Akima stopped when everyone appeared to be slathered, but Stith took continued satisfaction in spraying the remainder of the crowd. The aliens scrambled about angrily, slipping on the foam, turning on one another.

Akima shouted down in the loudest, most booming voice she could manage, "That gel is a special Human formulation, designed to stop armies in their tracks. If you don't wash it off within twenty minutes, the foam will harden into a polymer concrete. You won't be able to move. You'll become statues, and the only way to get it off will be to rip away the outer layers of your skin, or exoskeleton, or whatever you have."

This news threw the mob into a complete panic. Some fled immediately; others shouted their disbelief, but were soon overwhelmed by the wave of retreating, angry victims. The murderous crowd dissipated within moments, like an ice cube in lava.

Akima grinned. Stith looked down in surprise at the splattered, stained docking pad all around the ship. She saw plenty of footsteps and dropped weapons, but no enemies.

Unable to believe his eyes, Ishaq blinked again in astonishment. "Akima, how do you know what that stuff does? As a matter of fact, wasn't it dangerous to use?" He quickly wiped some foam flecks off his own hand.

"It's just a fire extinguisher, Ishaq, nothing more," she said. "But since that mob thinks we're such monsters, they were ready to believe anything."

The young man laughed. "Well, at least that got rid of them for now."

"They'll be back, don't doubt it," Stith said. Her triangular eyes glowed yellow. "Jaxor was willing to break his own rules—gave away the confidential location of our ship on the docking field. What's to stop him from sending his mob to destroy your father's cultural storage unit?"

Ishaq looked green at hearing the frightening possibility. Akima hardened her expression. "We'll just have to prevent them from doing that."

In the high tower back at the Fauldro Flight Academy, Chancellor Jaxor's offices commanded a view that spread across the spacecraft hangars and endless, neatly arranged rows of storage cubicles.

But he paid no heed to the view when he returned to his tower, both exhilarated and infuriated from his experience at the Human's ship. What caught his full attention was the ominous figure lounging in the plush chair by the chancellor's desk, with all four arms crossed and overlapped on his gray chest.

"And did it work?" Golbus said.

Jaxor looked in dismay at the crime lord from Solbrecht and took a small retreating step toward the door. But he knew he couldn't run. Golbus always found a way to punish failures, but he never did so with his bare hands. He devised more subtle, more *painful* ways.

"Not . . . exactly, Lord Golbus. I'm still working on the problem."

"How much of a *problem* is there to work on?" the crime lord said. "I am personally uneasy about the prospect of Drej coming to Fauldro. The Humans have been too obvious here, flaunting their presence."

"But, My Lord, there are very few Humans on—"

"One Human is too many when it comes to my business interests," Golbus snapped. "This Human female, Akima, has already proved herself most troublesome, and I demand my vengeance on her."

"I . . . tried to incite the mob, My Lord," the chancellor said. "But the Humans had . . . unpleasant weapons on their ship. I'm sure hundreds are dead. The Humans and that Mantrin weapons specialist attacked us. They slaughtered the mob, coating them with a polymer cement that is sure to suffocate and kill all of its victims within the hour."

Golbus frowned. "And have you ever heard of this polymer cement before? What kind of weapon is it?"

"I'm sure it's some kind of *Human* invention, sir."

"I see, but I don't believe it for an instant," Golbus said, unfolding his arms like a demi-spider. "The Drej have already attacked a Drifter colony. Obviously, they have returned from their years of dormancy intending to hunt down the remaining Humans. I have a deep and abiding horror for those aliens, and I don't want to draw their attention. If that means exterminating any Humans I encounter, then it must be done."

"Of course," Jaxor said. "It must be done."

"And not just Human individuals—*anything* that

smacks of Earth: culture or history or possessions. Something about the Human race forced the Drej to take extreme action." He tapped a datascreen on the chancellor's cluttered desktop. "I've been going through all of Fauldro's documentation, and I've found something very interesting."

Jaxor was alarmed. "But, sir, that data is completely confidential. Fauldro's business rests on this—"

"Confidentiality is irrelevant when it comes to Humans! Nothing matters when it comes to Humans." Golbus swiveled the thin screen and pointed to an entry. "I have found a large storage container holding thousands of Human artifacts. It's been here for ten years, and I'm certain this is what the Drej would be after if they came here. Who knows—they could be on their way at this instant!"

He pounded both sets of fists down on the desktop. "We must destroy this hoard so the Drej will have no reason to come here. I have countless investments on Fauldro, and I don't intend to see them ruined."

Golbus smiled with his wrinkly, grayish lips, imagining how satisfying revenge would be against the ones who had duped him on Solbrecht. "You must try again, Jaxor," he said. Then he cracked his numerous knuckles. "And this time, destroy all their precious cultural items. Those can't be replaced. You can kill the specific Humans later on."

It was after dark by the time Jaxor got back to work. He called up business associates and cashed in favors to arrange as many angry and malleable spectators as possible.

Lurking unseen in the chancellor's tower offices, Golbus also worked on the communication channels, summoning mercenaries, bounty hunters, and strong-arm companions of various black marketeers. He would hire them all. This second time, the defenders of Fauldro would not be so easily cowed. They would have better weapons, and some of them would act as de facto leaders, with a plan and a strategy.

This time, Jaxor made certain that his voice boomed even louder from the speakers installed around the square. After several minutes of surly insults and yelling, the vigilantes were whipped into a frenzy, convinced that extreme violence was the only solution.

Most races living on Fauldro had never seen the color of Human blood, but tonight they would satisfy their curiosity.

"You must destroy the tainted Human presence!" Jaxor shouted. "Wipe out any evidence of their evil artifacts. As a heinous provocation, we know they have secretly hidden a storage container here among our valuable items. If the Drej attack Fauldro, all of *your* most valuable possessions will be destroyed along with those of the Humans." He let the angry echoes reverberate through the crowd. Jaxor lowered his voice to a growl. "This insidious tactic shows how low Humans will stoop. Only if we obliterate all remnants of Earth and the Human race will we ourselves be safe from the Drej."

Several mob members fired blasters into the air. The energy bolts blazed like celebratory fireworks in the gloomy evening skies. Then, with Jaxor leading them, the violent crowd marched toward the labyrinth of storage units, ready to crush and burn all memories of Earth.

-18-

I t was time to do something.

In the *Ronin*, Akima considered her companions, tapping a finger to her lips. She, Ishaq, and Stith stood alone against a world of prejudice, an angry population who wanted to destroy them. The odds could have been worse, she supposed, but not by much.

Ishaq looked distraught. "My father and his Titan team risked their lives to gather all those things while Earth was being evacuated." He looked earnestly at Akima. "Those cultural treasures are worth more than any one person, than any of our lives."

"Hey, let's not get carried away, kid," Stith said.

But Ishaq wrung his slender hands. "They're not just objects—they are the best tangible things that remain of Human civilization and achievement. If Jaxor and his zealots destroy them, they'll erase the greatest gift that Human beings have to offer the galaxy."

Akima didn't argue with the young man, though with

the current downtrodden state of humanity, she wondered whether anyone in the Spiral Arm would ever be interested in those artistic gifts. But her grandmother had taught her to value such precious objects. For years, Akima had kept a baseball, a perfume bottle, postcards—and the items in the storage container were worth far more than any of her personal keepsakes.

"All right, practical lesson. Obviously we can't unload *everything* and move it somewhere safer." Stith paced the deck, considering possibilities. "We could fly the *Ronin* over there and have Ishaq pick a few of the best items. No sense wasting time. It's probably all we can salvage before the mob gets to the storage unit."

Akima raised her eyebrows. "You're thinking too small, Stith. I was planning to move the entire storage container. Take it somewhere out of reach."

The weapons specialist's tail thrashed, and she reared back. "Well, kid, I suppose that's another option." She took large steps toward the cockpit, then looked over her shoulder. "I take it you know a way to implement this plan of yours?"

Akima rubbed her hands together, ready for action. "Just leave it to me, but I might need a little time. You two will have to delay the mob if they come too soon."

Stith's sharp mouth curved in a smile, showing all of her teeth. "All right. You leave *that* to me."

As nightfall tinted the Fauldro sky an indigo purple, Akima raised the ship up on its maneuvering engines and arrowed out toward the immense maze of the warehouse district. She followed the grid on her map which Ishaq had marked to indicate the position of Mohammed's secret cultural storehouse. They wouldn't have a little blinking scutbot to guide them this time.

As they passed over the populated sectors of the city, she looked down with dismay to see crowds of people already streaming in their direction. The angry attackers took hoverscooters and small vehicles; all the company guards had abandoned their posts and left the gates wide open, no doubt following orders from Jaxor.

Even when viewed from a height, the rallying creatures obviously carried real and ominous weapons slung over their shoulders this time. One of the angry aliens fired into the sky at their ship as it passed overhead. Akima wasn't sure the rowdy creature intended to target the Human vessel, or if he was just in the mood to cause some damage. Stith wanted to set an example by turning him into a blot of grease-stained smoke on the pavement, but Akima flew out of range before the weapons specialist could decide which blaster to use.

Akima flew over the uneven rooftops and stacked units. Below, the famed storage maze of Fauldro looked like a hive constructed by drunken insects. Large containers and small lay stacked and arranged, seemingly at random. Some were boobytrapped and surrounded by defensive fields; others appeared battered and dilapidated, as if scavengers had already stolen every item of value from inside. Something about the rundown-looking ones, though, made Akima suspect that these containers might be even more dangerous or valuable, a clever disguise to trick would-be thieves into thinking nothing of worth remained there.

They had pulled ahead of the surging, club-wielding mob making its way to the supposedly confidential location; Akima knew Chancellor Jaxor must have been perfectly happy to surrender the secret. The glowing path on the ground-navigation map blinked as they closed in on the indicated circle. "We're almost there!" Ishaq said. "I recognize this area."

All of the squarish cubicles looked alike to Akima, though. She tried to imagine how long Mohammed Bourain had searched for a place to store his treasures after the destruction of Earth, how he had gone about buying an armored cargo pod with a reinforced hatch. He and any other survivors from his Titan cultural team would have placed their hopes in this cache, praying it would survive until Sam Tucker succeeded in finding a new world for the Human race.

For the year she had lived with Mohammed on New Marrakech, he had guarded the secret of his dream, protected the location of these artifacts, hoping that one day he or his son would be called on to bring back all of the cultural treasures. Akima wasn't about to let some wild-eyed, bigoted chancellor on an alien world destroy humanity's legacy.

She took the ship down with a gentle blast of reverse thrusters, zeroing in on the nondescript cubicle that held so much of value. Though this storage unit looked the same as all the others, Akima didn't believe for a moment that Jaxor's howling mob would be unable to find it.

Akima settled the *Ronin* down on the broad metal roof of the storage chamber, but left the engines running. Ishaq and Stith hurried to the exit hatch. The weapons specialist carried a large crate that contained a selection of her favorite destructive tools. "Be prepared," Stith said, as if expressing a personal motto.

"I think you've got about an hour until they get here,"

Akima said. "Do what you can to set up some defenses. I have to fly to the academy to pick up a . . . piece of equipment. I'll be back as soon as I can."

Ishaq looked troubled to see her leave, but he swallowed hard and nodded. Akima looked over to Stith, who was obviously spoiling for the fight. "You think you can handle this, Stith?"

The weapons specialist cracked her knuckles, bounced experimentally on her triple-jointed legs, then looked down at her sharp, clawed fingers. "This is my specialty."

Akima waved farewell to her companions. "I'll trust in your daring strategy, Stith, but don't short-change Ishaq. He might be more help than you realize."

The young man raised his hand. "We'll hold down the fort, but hurry back. And stay *alive*."

"Nothing I can't handle," Akima assured him with a brave smile. She certainly hoped it was the truth.

The *Ronin* rose away into the night, streaking off toward the Fauldro piloting school. She took one last look behind her to see the two small figures of her friends entering the storage container and sealing it so they could set to work on their preparations.

Akima vowed that she would make it back here before the whole place went up in flames.

—19—

Stith knew exactly what they needed to do, but they had to work fast.

Ishaq raced around inside the storage container, making sure that all of the vents and hatches were locked down and sealed. Stith marched after him, welding the metal hinges with a small hand blaster as an added precaution. Nobody was going to get inside here without cutting through the walls.

Unfortunately, Jaxor and his mob were probably capable of doing just that.

Stith took a lift platform to the top of the large cargo unit and crawled onto the rooftop. Her big legs barely fit through the round-edged hatch, which had been designed for Human-sized (or smaller) creatures. Stith's tail twitched and clanged like a sledgehammer on top of the unit's roof.

She scanned the nearby warehouse containers and the mosaic streets below, segmented walkways that were not only meant to be attractive, but also designed to help locate complex addresses.

Ishaq climbed up beside her and stood on the metal roof, his face ashen. "I've done all I could to secure this unit, but it doesn't seem like enough. Are you rigging up other defenses?"

"I'm getting to that, kid." She continued to study her surroundings and think strategically. Musing, she gestured to the adjacent storage unit, an armored box with small identification designs on each side. The hatches and lids didn't look very secure. "See that container? Those markings?"

Ishaq looked at the triangle design and nodded. "Yeah, I've seen hundreds of them. They're all over the place in the storage sector. Does it mean anything special?"

"Absolutely not," Stith said. "In fact, you might even consider those units . . . expendable."

Ishaq's eyes widened. "Why? What does the triangle marking mean?"

"Those units are Hodrian, probably full of memory spheres."

Seeing Ishaq's puzzled expression, Stith crouched and sprang across the gap with her powerful leg muscles. After spreading her wide, three-toed feet, she landed hard on the roof of the other container. With a swift kick of her armored foot, she broke open the barely secured roof hatch.

"Full, just like I expected," she called over. Stith stretched her arm down into the open hole and withdrew several small glass spheres, each about the size of an eyeball.

She bounded back across, waving her tail for balance,

while Ishaq skittered out of the way so the Mantrin could land. Stith held out the little glass spheres, and Ishaq picked them up. Each one was perfectly transparent, containing a scrap of papery material on which something had been scrawled in a strange language.

"Memory spheres, like I said." Stith picked one up and scrutinized it. "The Hodrians believe that each person exists only so long as his name is remembered. So they keep track of every member of their race who has ever lived, one name sealed inside each one of these spheres."

Under the dim, pinkish-yellow light of glowpanels that illuminated the nighttime warehouse districts, she could read the carefully written name. "*Reminat Janush*. I have no idea who he was, but here he's still remembered." Stith flicked the ball with her long finger, and it sailed in a perfect arc to plunk into the open hole on the roof of the Hodrian storage container.

"Because the Hodrians are an old race, they've filled their own planet with those memory spheres, piling them in wells and canyons and landfills until now they've had to rent storage containers all over Fauldro just to hold the names of their people." The weapons specialist shook her head and lowered her voice to a growl. "If you ask me, it'd be easier if they just didn't *breed* so much."

"But how does that help us?" Ishaq said, watching the distant lights move closer. "They're just names inside little glass balls."

Stith gave him a sidelong glance. "We'll just have to use our imaginations, won't we? Got a few other ideas, too."

• • •

It was fully dark by the time the mob finally arrived, and Stith was ready.

She remained on the rooftop of the thick-walled container, out of range of hurled rocks, but still vulnerable to a well-placed blaster shot. She hoped the violence wouldn't come to that.

Stith and Ishaq heard the yelling and cursing first, then weapons banging against storage container walls as the rioters pushed forward. The crowd streamed through narrow, labyrinthine streets and approached the broad, clear flagstones in front of the big armored container.

When they saw Stith standing like an ominous gargoyle on the roof, the group let out a howl of anger. Chancellor Jaxor, naturally, was at the rear of the group, urging them on, shouting through his loudspeaker.

Ishaq ducked down beside Stith on the rooftop, and she pushed him forcefully back through the ceiling hatch where he would be safe among the cultural artifacts of Earth. But he popped his head and shoulders out again, more worried about the artifacts than his own safety. The young man continued scanning the skies, hoping to see Akima return with the promised rescue ship. The sky remained clear, studded with moving blips of satellites and far-distant stars.

But no large ship approached.

Stith sneered at the well-armed crowds nudging one another along and finding shared courage in their actions and shouted comments. "Look at you! You're all insults to your respective races—attacking Humans in hopes of saving your own cowardly hides! Couldn't Jaxor find a more impressive bunch of losers to solve his problems for him?"

Someone hurled a stone, but it flew so far from its target that Stith heard it clank against the end of the cargo unit behind her.

"Human lover!" somebody shouted.

A slightly more reasonable voice called, "Come on down from there. We're only after the *Humans* and their treasures."

A third voice added, "Yeah! We need to keep ourselves safe. The Drej are coming. If they find anything from Earth, they'll destroy us all."

Stith said, "I'm sure the Drej could find other excuses to destroy this place if they wanted to . . . like your lack of brains, for instance."

The mob howled and then rushed forward.

"Touchy, touchy," Stith muttered, inwardly glad that they were so predictable. The crowd charged ahead, yelling, raising their clubs, shaking their fists . . . right into the trap.

During the hour they'd had to prepare, Ishaq and Stith had removed several of the large flagstones in front of Mohammed's storage unit. They imaged the shapes and textures with small holoprojectors, then rigged up a perfect illusion that showed no difference from the rest of the street surface. Yet the holograms covered gaping, open holes that Stith had filled with barrels of dirty, used lubricants and greasy lumps of sludge destined for industrial recycler stations.

The first aliens raced forward, intending to hammer Mohammed's armored storage unit. Instead, when they stepped on the illusory flagstones, they fell up to their necks (unfortunately, some of the species were shorter than that) into thick, multicolored goop. The noxious substance clung to their fur or feathers or scales, drenching them in foul smells and thick slime.

Stith couldn't stop laughing as the creatures at the rear of the group, eager to do damage, continued pushing forward even as the front rows flailed their arms and tentacles trying to avoid falling into the trap. More victims were pushed into the disguised holes, crawling over each other, trailing smears of slippery muck across the ground. Finally, the angry crowd swirled around and avoided the booby-trapped sections.

"That stuff isn't toxic, is it?" Ishaq asked her. "Will it wash off?"

Stith shrugged. "In a few weeks. Might take off a few layers of skin . . . but skin grows back."

Ishaq didn't object to the big Mantrin's tactics. He just looked overhead again, searching desperately for Akima. . . .

Before the mob could regain its momentum, Stith opened a pouch at her side and withdrew several squishy packets, each labeled differently.

Ishaq looked at her. "What are those?"

"Plan B, for tonight." Stith handed one to him. "Pheromone packets, keyed to the various alien races you see. I picked the most common species . . . and I think it'll spark a little party down there."

"What do you mean?" Ishaq asked, and turned the gelatinous object in his hand.

"Careful not to break that," Stith said. "Many species use certain chemicals and scents during mating season. It's meant to drive potential partners wild. When we throw those packets out into the crowd, we'll be increasing the sex appeal of a lot of our attackers—but not necessarily for the correct species. We're about to throw a bit of confusion into their ranks."

"You mean—?" Ishaq said.

"Exactly," she answered. "Stith's dating service, coming right up." The weapons specialist tossed one of the packets into a random clot of aliens. It burst upon impact, splattering a perfumy substance onto several of them. Ishaq hurled his in a different direction.

Stith soon emptied her pouch of pheromone packets and watched swirling knots of movement among the mob members. Some aliens sniffed the air, pushing others away to get to the source of the alluring scents. Competing aliens fought with them, struggling over their instinctive choice of a mate, though the pheromones frequently had them completely confused.

Aliens of some species drew back, immune to the scents but wary because of the holographically disguised sludge pits. They did not understand the nature of Stith's pheromone assault.

While a percentage of the attackers gathered around the amorous distractions, the rest pushed forward again, gingerly stepping around the sludge traps. Stith had added one or two muck pits closer to the main hatch, and the mob members soon discovered those . . . by falling in.

"Uh, do we happen to have a Plan C?" Ishaq said. "They're almost to the front access door."

"Plan C, coming up." Stith withdrew the hand blaster with which she had melted the inside locks. "Don't ask for a Plan D. I only had an hour to set up, you know."

She pointed the blaster, and Ishaq cringed, thinking she might start mowing down their attackers. Instead, with one blast she melted off the hinges and locking hatch of the nondescript old Hodrian storage container.

With a groan, the heavy metal plate in front shifted and slid, then finally dropped down as the frenzied aliens scrambled to get out of the way to avoid being squashed. As the container broke open, thousands—then millions— of the tiny glass balls spilled out, a raging flood of transparent marbles that spewed across the flagstone streets and ricocheted down the alleyways.

Some of the closer rioters were swept off their feet or tentacles, bowled over by an avalanche of names encased in glass. Within moments, the flood of name balls spread, branching out and knocking over even the pheromone-dizzied aliens.

Far behind, Jaxor stood atop one of the smaller storage containers and yowled in anger. But the strewn Hodrian memory spheres continued to bounce and roll, breaking the mob into a tangle of arms and legs and other limbs. A roar went up as toppling aliens knocked others backward into the sludge pits again.

Stith shook with laughter again. "Those Hodrians may be long dead, but they've finally done something memorable."

In her heart, though, she knew this would only delay the attack . . . and probably not long enough. She nudged Ishaq back down through the roof hatch and climbed inside after him.

Stith reached over her head and dragged the metal hatch back into place, sealing and locking it. She looked down at the wealth of carefully packaged sculptures, paintings, recording disks, and original manuscripts.

"Hey, kid, while we wait, should we listen to some of that famous Earth music?" she asked Ishaq.

He raised his eyebrows, surprised at the suggestion.

"My father always liked to play Mozart during times of tension."

"Perfect time, then. I've never heard anything from this composer you revere so much. I'm sure I'll find it relaxing."

Within moments, faster than Stith had expected, they heard pounding sounds, clanging and hammering, as the mob battered the walls of the sealed cargo container. She could hear the throb and drone of their chanting, their angry howls.

After being humiliated repeatedly, the rioters were out for blood now, not just destruction.

Trying to ignore the hammering sounds, Ishaq did play a piece of classical music, "Confutatis" from Mozart's *Requiem*, a dramatic and heroic movement that Stith found stirring.

The mob clamored louder. She knew that the thick, armored walls wouldn't last long once the attackers brought high-powered blasters and torches to bear against the doors. Stith didn't want to admit that she was growing very nervous.

Mozart's music was soothing in its own way, but she would have been better able to relax if she had known how close Akima was.

—20—

If Akima could fly the fastest and hottest fighter craft at the Fauldro piloting school, she figured she could handle a bulky cargo hauler, even with its cumbersome maneuvering. The craft would be much bigger than she was accustomed to, but the controls were simple, designed for dockworkers and crate handlers rather than sophisticated pilots like herself.

When she reached the fenced gate of the academy landing field, Akima was relieved to find that her passcard still functioned. She had feared Jaxor might have canceled her student access, but the anti-Human chancellor had been too busy inciting a riot to tend to such small details.

After this evening, she would make the chancellor happy by never returning here again. Before that, Akima meant to prove to Jaxor that she was full of surprises. The fiberfence gates rattled aside, allowing her to hurry through the dark barricades toward the night-drenched landing field.

Ahead, bathed in low-spectrum docking lights, several battered cargo haulers sat parked next to refueling bays. Equipped with heavy tractor beams, they had been put to recent hard service during the removal of all storage units leased by the Rutan Conglomeration.

When the Rutani had decided to withdraw their business from the Fauldro warehousing district, the vessels had worked round the clock. Most of the crews were now exhausted and taking a day off to celebrate their overtime wages or simply sleep. Akima guessed that no one would notice another cargo hauler taking off into the night. After recent events, that occurrence would be seen as nothing unusual.

Easy pickings, Akima thought.

On nimble feet, she raced across the open pavement, trying not to look suspicious. After leaving Stith and Ishaq behind at the cultural storehouse, she knew she had to hurry. Even the Mantrin weapons specialist couldn't hold out for long against Jaxor's mob.

The old-model cargo hauler stood like a giant, ugly box with protruding thrusters and attitude-control jets. Akima should have been ashamed to fly something so completely nonaerodynamic, so utterly ungraceful. But she wasn't here to show off. She needed to rescue her friends and all of Earth's surviving treasures.

The side of the dented metal hull bore letters in a language that Akima did not recognize. Judging from the hauler's appearance, though, the hulk deserved a name something along the lines of *Roadkill Sloth*.

Oh, well, as long as the engines started . . .

She activated the outer hatch and climbed into the hauler's ridiculously small piloting compartment. It smelled of multispecies body odors, as well as old polymer coatings on the seats, overheated poured-resin control panels, and singed insulation. Maintenance on cargo haulers was apparently not one of Fauldro's priorities.

She powered on the control systems and popped in her student training card. The card allowed her automatic access to all vehicles, since the chief instructor, Herkimer Fhlax, often assigned them whatever flying wrecks he could find. Even if the piloting school did post guards, who would dream a student would be crazy enough to hijack a sluggish, ugly cargo hauler?

She noted that the cargo bay indicator read EMPTY, exactly as she'd hoped. The bottom jaws would open up and powerful tractor beams could wrench Mohammed's loaded storage container out of its anchorage. Akima would fly off while drawing it up into the hauler's belly. Then the powerful but clunky craft could take them into orbit, off to someplace safe . . . wherever that might be. Unfortunately, though, that meant leaving the *Ronin* here.

She called up a map grid on the smeary, crackling screen and selected the address for Mohammed's storage unit, which allowed her to set an appropriate course. Then the automated hauler could do the rest.

The workhorse engines sputtered and wheezed, but Akima pounded on the control panel with a growl that would have made Stith proud. The frustrated gesture worked surprisingly well. The underbelly thrusters spouted heavy steam, and the ship wobbled upward against Fauldro's gravity like a huge, drunken bumblebee.

But the feel of motion exhilarated Akima, the thrum of the engines, the lumbering weight of the cargo hauler as it plowed through the air. She cruised over the landing field's perimeter fences, straining hard against the altitude levers to raise the vessel high enough so that it didn't clip its bottom hull against the fiberfence barricades.

The shadowy forms of two guards near the fence raised segmented insectile arms in the air, shaking fists at her . . . but Akima didn't think they were sounding an alarm. The guards just didn't like her flying so low overhead and disturbing their evening conversation.

Akima flew safely beyond the spaceport perimeter. "This just might work after all."

"She'll never get away with it," Golbus growled as he stared through the observation windows in Chancellor Jaxor's tower. In disbelief, he watched the clumsy cargo hauler weave and sway, gaining altitude and speed as it cleared the fence.

Golbus had been lurking in the shadows of the isolated office, taking command of Jaxor's files so he could ponder other work, other schemes that needed to be completed. The crime lord had always kept a low profile on Fauldro, though his multiple hands were involved in many businesses here. He controlled numerous illegal activities not only on Solbrecht, but in dozens of other systems as well.

Few off-worlders knew his identity. That was the best way to retain a position of authority.

Chancellor Jaxor was a fool, but Golbus could easily twist him to do whatever he wished so he allowed the head of the Flight Academy to believe he was a trusted colleague. Golbus had already set up a few contingency plans, ready to squash the weakling Jaxor the moment he failed in his duties. Successors waited in the wings, and it wouldn't take long to find a replacement, someone who would be deliriously grateful to Golbus for his new position.

But as he sat alone in the dim tower office, scanning to find ways that Jaxor had been cheating him, Golbus had looked up to see the running lights activate on a cargo hauler that was not scheduled to make any runs.

He had been dismayed at the loss of so much business when the Rutan Conglomeration had pulled out all of their storage cubicles. Now the Hodrians were making similar threats, although there weren't enough storage planets in the galaxy to hold the memory spheres of all their offspring. Golbus had been considering whether he could sell the Hodrians a new technique for imprinting names on tiny microdots so each glass sphere could hold several generations of an entire extended family. . . .

However, the cargo ship's departure had interrupted this entrepreneurial train of thought. Golbus called up the data listing scheduled flights and hauler requests and discovered that the ship lifting off below was not authorized to go anywhere.

It took him a few moments to access the docking records and the readout, all four of his hands pounding on keypads, until he discovered the identity of the pilot who had used a card to activate the hauler engines. *A student card!*

Golbus squinted, unable to believe that one of the trainees from Jaxor's precious academy would be so audacious. Was it a prank? Hotshot trainees often dared each other to do stupid things.

But then he saw the student number, cross-checked it with an identity roster, and recognized the name. *Akima!* The Human pilot who had already caused him so much trouble. She was stealing a hauler!

Jaxor was supposed to be leading a mob right now to destroy the Human artifacts, to wipe out all traces of the Earthlings and their possessions. What if the Drej were coming? What if the aliens were on their way even now, scanning Fauldro, picking up signals. . . .

What did Akima think she was doing with a hauler? He raced back to the tower window and stared out, watching the lights of the vessel recede. *She'll never get away with it.*

He found the public address system for the student barracks on the academy grounds. He switched on the ALL CALL button and bellowed down, startling any creatures who might be resting or amusing themselves in their quarters. If Glk had done his recruiting job well enough, these eager fresh pilots would be ready to follow orders.

"Attention, all pilots. We have an emergency. All trainees scramble to your ships. Your fellow student, the Human Akima, is stealing a cargo hauler. You must prevent this illegal act."

From the barracks, one gruff-voiced trainee shouted at the loudspeaker. "Identify yourself, sir."

"Never mind my identification," Golbus said, wondering why they weren't rushing to their ships to chase the Human criminal. Hadn't they heard him?

"Then I'm afraid I don't recognize your authority, sir," said the gruff student.

Golbus wished he knew the name of this annoying rebel. He had little experience in being disobeyed. "My name is Golbus, and I believe several of you have signed on to work for me when you receive your certificates." He let that hang for a moment. "I speak with the authority of Chancellor Jaxor. Whoever is *not* at the landing field, at their ships, ready for pursuit within the next five minutes will be immediately expelled from the school. And don't think I won't carry out that threat. You can forget about being employed in my organization, or any other."

He switched off the intercom, paused a moment, and then sounded the alarms for good measure. There, that would rouse them.

Golbus went to the window and saw figures racing across the landing field pavement, some tugging on flight suits, others flopping empty sleeves behind them as they hurried to the available craft.

Akima's cargo hauler had puttered off, swaying in the air as if it could barely hold itself up even with an empty cargo hold. Below, the first of the pursuing fighters powered up engines and then flared off, streaking across the landing field.

It was Dhornan. Golbus had checked the records. He was the top student in the class, except for when Akima occasionally outsmarted him.

Against such competition, Golbus knew she didn't have a chance.

When the first warning shots seared the cargo hauler's hull, alarm lights blazed across her control panel. Akima was already having enough trouble just trying to maneuver the big ship. She had her hands full with the controls, fighting against winds, unable to dodge or fly graceful courses as she would have preferred. "Okay, it's a challenge," she muttered. "I can handle it."

And Herkimer Fhlax had said those Sandor Gammas didn't maneuver well! She snorted in disgust.

Now, with other students streaking through the air and closing the distance, she tried to think of a way to outsmart them, especially while trapped in this big lunk of a vehicle. She had hoped to be a bit more subtle with her plan, sneaking away and slipping off with Mohammed's whole storage container without causing an undue amount of trouble.

"But you had to make it complicated," Akima muttered, not sure who to blame, but willing to accept any scapegoat she could find.

The lead pursuit craft roared past her, then streaked across her bow, weaving sharp wings to scrape a warning signature of ionized air across her path. She recognized the craft, knew the pilot.

It would be Dhornan, her tall and quiet rival.

She had bested the grim, silent alien student several times. Though the reserved creature had never made overt threats, had never even spoken more than a sentence to her, Akima did not doubt that he meant to best her this time and reclaim his position.

Akima didn't care. She'd let him have the title so long as she could keep the cargo hauler. But she doubted Dhornan would ever make such a bargain. The ethereal amphibian was relentless and driven, willing to take risks, but never willing to give up. Not unlike Akima herself. . . .

Akima was confident that she could outfly all the other trainees in the class even in this sluggish monstrosity. But Dhornan was another story entirely.

Gathering her wits about her, breathing deeply to increase her awareness, Akima concentrated on her every move. With full, wobbly thrust, she took the cargo hauler off to the south, trying to escape her pursuers.

Back in the storage labyrinth, Ishaq and Stith would just have to hold out for a little while longer. . . .

–21–

H eart thudding in her chest, palms sweating, peripheral vision tracking twenty different sets of readouts simultaneously, Akima tore through the skies of Fauldro, wresting every possible drop of speed and maneuverability from the cargo hauler.

"Okay, *Roadkill*, let's move it," she urged the ship.

Akima did not have to remind herself that this was no mere maneuver, not simply a showcase for her abilities. She was flying for her life today—and far more. Ishaq and Stith were depending on her, but she had a greater responsibility as well. Collectively, the treasures Mohammed's team had hidden represented the cultural heart of Earth, the memory of her people, perhaps the very soul of humanity.

A love for these things had been part of her grandmother's legacy to Akima. Preserving the heritage for all to share had been Mohammed's dream. Regardless of what happened to her, Akima could not allow those precious artifacts to be lost forever.

As her cargo hauler plodded on, dodging fire from Dhornan and two other pursuers, she felt a stab of disappointment. During her time at the Fauldro Flight Academy, she had hoped that her obvious skills and dedication would win her a few friends among her classmates. She had been willing to endure the relentless teasing and stupid jokes, trying to be good-natured. Now, all she could tell for sure was that somebody—presumably Golbus—wanted her dead. And her own classmates were willing to help him achieve his goal.

As if to emphasize the point, a blaster shot from Dhornan's craft pounded the hauler's rear engine pod.

"High road, Akima," she reminded herself through gritted teeth. Her mission was too important. She had no time for thoughts of fear, self-pity, or disappointment. She had to compartmentalize, impose order on her troubled thoughts. She set aside the smallest possible corner of her mind and ruthlessly smashed all personal feelings of fear, panic, sadness, and disappointment into it. She assigned a larger portion of her brain to analyzing the data that was coming from her control-panel readouts.

Another segment of her mind launched itself forward to plan an escape once she had reached Ishaq and Stith. But by far the largest part of her mind was dedicated to the here and now, analyzing her course and her options even as she dodged enemy fire. She set the remaining segment of her brain running through comparisons between the cargo hauler and every other type of vessel she had ever studied, looking for tricks and maneuvers she might use to outwit her classmates.

For a time Akima managed to hold her own, but it

was an uphill battle. When she plunged into a heavy dive, rolled like a whale in the sky, and then pulled out in a clumsy ascent, she noted with grim satisfaction that one of her fellow pilots lost control of his vessel completely and was forced to eject. The attack craft hit the surface and exploded in a satisfying puff of orange flame.

After several more desperate maneuvers, Akima's cargo hauler had begun to outdistance two of the other pilots as well. No matter what she did, however, she could not shake Dhornan. He was the best.

He followed, trick for trick, maneuver for maneuver, always gaining on her. She groaned. "If I had known being number one meant that much to you, I might have let you win more often. But not this time."

Realizing she didn't have much time, Akima attempted her most daring tactic yet. Between two tall, monolithic towers just inside the gigantic storage district, the winds of Fauldro whistled constantly. Her instructors had called it a prime navigation hazard, and Herkimer Fhlax had taken great pleasure in making sure every student crashed there at least once in their simulator training. The heavy wind currents were like whitewater rapids in the air, treacherous and unpredictable.

Akima headed there.

She was willing to bet no one had ever tried this maneuver in a military-class XR400 or a even a Condor Skimmer with double ion engines—much less in a heavy cargo hauler. But this beast had a lot of momentum and wouldn't easily be slapped around by the ferocious gusts.

Her cargo hauler plunged between the giant towers, fighting the torrents of air, with Dhornan right on her tail. Her massive craft swayed as the breezes hit her broadside, but she somehow maintained stability in her unlikely steed. After riding the current for several seconds, she broke out of the vortex and righted herself, soaring onward. The exertion, both mental and physical, had been tremendous, but she had succeeded.

Behind her, Dhornan's smaller attack craft spun and swirled like a bit of chaff in a tornado. She increased her lead, knowing he couldn't follow her, but hoping he at least wouldn't crash and burn.

And then her rival pulled it off.

Dhornan's ship escaped the wind's clutches and reoriented itself. Akima groaned and tried to think fast. She had used her best best tricks, but she'd have to come up with a new one. Unfortunately, that desperate maneuver had cost her time.

Now she saw with even greater dismay that the other two remaining pursuers, seeing her ploy with the tower winds, had circled on a safer, longer route, and now came around like a closing trap.

With Dhornan coming from behind, she flew straight ahead, ready to ram the other two out of the sky. At least the cargo hauler had plenty of mass. When the oncoming ships were within weapons range again, she found herself forced to dodge their fire. She saw that she could not gain altitude, since Dhornan's fighter craft now flew directly above her and parallel to her course.

Below, in the cluttered warehouse district, she had no room to dive, especially not in such a cumbersome vessel. With the two oncoming pilots' shots bracketing her on either side, Akima had no place left to fly. A cargo hauler wasn't armed, so she couldn't even fire a shot in her own defense, nor could she simply outrun them.

Steeling herself to do the best she could in a bad situation, Akima banked, described a wide circle in the air, and headed straight toward the other two pilots again. Above her, Dhornan banked on a parallel course. She saw his weapons warming up, glowing hot.

Then Dhornan fired—but not at her. Amazingly, he targeted the oncoming ships.

One of the attack craft spun out, its engines disabled. The second pursuing ship pulled up and circled around, trailing smoke. Stunned, Akima watched the talented pilot bring the ship back under control barely in time to make a rough but safe landing.

Through a haze of astonishment, Akima heard Dhornan's voice come over the secure channel on her comm system. "Let me take it from here, Akima. Find your friends and get off Fauldro as quickly as possible."

"But how . . . why?" Akima stammered.

"We are much more alike than you will ever know," Dhornan answered. "Though I have kept it from Fauldro records, I am a Qu'utian. My main planet and most of my race were also destroyed by the Drej. A few of my people survive, but they are hidden by a deadly asteroid field, the rubble of Qu'ut Prime. We need good pilots to navigate that hazard and trade in secret with outsiders."

Akima could hardly believe what she was hearing. "But you agreed to work for Golbus."

"I had my reasons for wanting a job with him," Dhornan said over the comm channel. "I despise the Drej as much as any being in the Spiral Arm can, but I needed the passcodes and clearances Golbus offered. However, now that he is targeting Humans, I cannot go along with it. If I did, I would be as bad as the Drej. Even fear cannot excuse attempts at genocide. I believe he was behind a great many of the evil happenings on Fauldro."

Absurdly, Akima blurted out the first words that came to mind. "So you really are my friend?"

Behind them, one of the lagging academy pilots came forward on an attack run, seeing what he thought was a clear, easy shot. A rasping trill came over the comm system: Dhornan's laugh, which she had never heard before. "I would prefer a living friend to a dead one, but unless you leave now . . ."

"Got it!" Akima said. She peeled out, away from Dhornan, away from the other attacker, deeper into the Fauldro storage district. "Thank you!"

It took less than half an hour for her to zero in on the correct area, using the coordinates locked into the cargo hauler. Luckily, much of that task was automated. Once in the correct vicinity, Akima found it simple enough to locate the mob that had gathered in the narrow alleys between the ancient armored containers. As her vessel roared past, she could see neither Stith nor Ishaq, and could only hope that they had retreated inside the warehouse itself while the angry aliens pounded on the walls.

Swooping down over the mob, Akima saw several creatures coming forward with cutting lasers and blast-torches to open the walls. With no time to lose, she locked the tractor beam on to the container.

The field pulsed, getting its invisible grip, and when she flew upward again, the power of the cargo hauler yanked the entire storage unit off the ground—with Stith and Ishaq inside, she hoped. As she climbed higher, the tractor beam drew the repository into the cargo hold.

Snug and safe. The lower bay doors groaned closed.

With Mohammed's storage unit tucked inside the cargo hauler, Akima streaked upward, away from Fauldro and into open space.

— 22 —

For the next two days, Akima flew them from system to system in the enormous cargo hauler, always ensuring that they were not being followed. The cargo hauler had few amenities, but plenty of space. Inside the gigantic hold, Mohammed's nondescript storage container gave them much with which to occupy themselves.

They never wanted to return to Fauldro. But they didn't know where to go now. Concerned that they had lost the *Ronin* forever, Akima promised herself that they would get it back. Somehow.

When they reached an outer cometary field in the DeBray System, they took refuge for a few days, lost in the forest of space-borne icebergs and snowballs. High above the plane of planetary orbits, with the DeBray sun merely a bright faraway dot, they reviewed their options and made plans for the future.

The three friends spent countless hours together

browsing through sculptures, paintings, literature, and histories, or listening to music and watching holographic performances of plays, operas, ballets, and comedies.

After watching a slapstick act, Stith shook her head and said, "Guess you have to understand a culture better before you get their humor. I've seen wars that were funnier."

Ishaq produced the holoscroll and the tiny Buddha sculpture his father had been clutching in the wreckage of their home on New Marrakech. "I suppose these really belong here," he said.

Akima withdrew a datacard from her possessions and placed it beside the other two items. "And this too."

Stith looked at the datacard, her big ears pricking with interest. Ishaq suddenly smiled, recognizing it. "You still have Sam Tucker's log!"

Akima sighed at the tragic memories it inspired. "*That* is the delivery I was picking up on the day that the Drej attacked New Marrakech. The final log of the Earth scientist Sam Tucker. Mohammed was so interested in what it might say, but after he died and the colony was ruined, it didn't seem as important anymore."

Ishaq swallowed several times and his voice sounded hoarse with emotion. "Of course, my father never got to listen to it."

"Neither did I," Akima admitted. She picked up the datacard and activated the message. "No better time than now." The three stepped back to watch the lost Earth scientist speak.

"Personal log: Sam Tucker of the Titan Project. It has only been a few months since the destruction of Earth, and the Drej are pursuing me relentlessly. Unless I can get to a friendly planet where I can hide, this may be my last log entry. If so, my friends, this is goodbye.

"But it's not the end. Remember, there's still hope for mankind. The Titan Project made sure of that. Each of you who had a part in it, protect whatever you have that belongs to humanity and preserve it for the future. When the time is right, mankind will have a new planet.

"Long before the Drej arrived, I made a map of a hiding place, and I've taken the original *Titan* there. Only a trusted few know where the map is. When the time comes, mankind will make a new beginning, and then all of you can bring the heritage of Earth together with the survivors of humanity so that they too can know hope for the future.

"Do not despair. This is only the beginning."

Akima switched off the datacard. "That's all there was." A faint smile touched the corners of her mouth. "I wish I could have met him." She tapped a finger against her lips. "But the Drej must have gotten him shortly after he recorded that."

"Sounds like he was quite a guy," Stith observed. "Great scientist, good planner, security-minded, real optimist—in spite of the Drej."

"But the Drej didn't get his work," Ishaq said. "If they had, they wouldn't still be picking on Humans, would they?"

"Probably not." Akima spread her arms wide to indicate the artifacts all around them. "Like it or not, in a way, we've all become part of the Titan Project ourselves."

"This is our responsibility now," Ishaq agreed.

Stith planted her fists on her muscular hips. "Then, as your weapons specialist and your de facto security chief, I suggest we find a really safe place to hide all of this until the rest of the Titan Project is ready for us."

"We can't go to a Drifter colony," Ishaq said. "The Drej are already attacking those."

"Well, I don't like the idea of hiding Earth's treasures in a cometary cloud," Stith said. "We can't keep an eye on the stuff here. Might get lost or smashed to smithereens. We gotta come up with a better plan."

"Nothing we can't handle, if we work together." Akima grinned. "I'm glad you're on our side, Stith. We could use more allies like you." She paused, looking from Ishaq to the big weapons specialist. "Come to think of it, that gives me an idea."

-23-

Throughout his crack training at Fauldro's piloting academy, the Qu'utian Dhornan had preferred to remain silent. He had lived his life as a hidden survivor of a civilization nearly destroyed by the Drej, and he had not called attention to his race for fear of the same prejudice the anti-Human mob had shown toward Akima. But Dhornan knew how to observe and to act without talking. He studied details and knew exactly how to set wheels in motion to accomplish what he wanted.

Now that he had completed the full course of instruction at Fauldro, he was capable of flying risky supply runs through the dangerous asteroid field, which was all that remained of Qu'ut Prime. The rest of Dhornan's race had gone into hiding, rebuilding their culture where it could not be seen by Drej scanners. The Qu'utians had always remained somewhat isolated, and thus few others remembered what his near-extinct race looked like. But he knew full well that hatred for the Drej could push people—like Chancellor Jaxor—in irrational directions.

And he also knew who had really been in charge of the criminal activities on Fauldro, who had really manipulated the destructive mob.

With his turnabout during the sky chase, Dhornan had already helped Akima and her partners escape. But, being a Qu'utian, he could not let injustice simply fade away, not when he could do something about it.

Working quickly and quietly before the uproar had even died down, he sent anonymous letters and unsigned transmissions. Dhornan submitted incriminating evidence to various commercial authorities and bureaucratic enforcers on Fauldro. Before anyone had noticed what he was doing, the corruption and crimes had been exposed for everyone to see.

Long ago, Chancellor Jaxor had filed documents personally vouching for Golbus as an upstanding citizen, a fine businessman whose workings could only benefit the overall prosperity of Fauldro. But Dhornan had discovered the true nature of the crime lord's work on Solbrecht. He did not hesitate to reveal Golbus's widespread criminal activities to all those in charge of processing permits and approving business plans.

Anyone in collusion with the Solbrecht crime lord would be in nearly as much trouble, and Fauldro's government wanted nothing to do with embarrassing revelations. It was bad for business.

Therefore, with so much of Fauldro's confidential storage business already in jeopardy, Chancellor Jaxor's fate was sealed. The fact that he had divulged confidential records now enraged many of the citizens who had taken part in the mob attack. The very same citizens called for the resignation of their public officials. The bureaucrats had no choice but to react swiftly and decisively. After imprisoning Jaxor, they censured Golbus and condemned his actions. They even issued warrants for his arrest, though Dhornan suspected Golbus would move too fast for the authorities.

When it was learned that Golbus himself had given the orders—completely unauthorized orders—for academy trainees to pursue Akima in her cargo hauler, Dhornan had faced no reprimands. Indeed, with Golbus and Jaxor out of the picture, no one had pressed the matter at all.

With cold, relentless precision, the Qu'utian pilot wrapped up his matters in preparation for returning to his Drej-ravaged home system. If he were a member of another species, he might have planned to remain on Fauldro just to gloat, to enjoy the discomfiture he had caused. But Qu'utians were not a spiteful race. Instead, he simply took satisfaction in knowing that he had done the right thing. Exposing all of the corruption might even make Fauldro a better, stronger society.

His work complete, Dhornan looked forward to going home.

Taking the fastest, most powerful ship he could find, Golbus flew away from Fauldro without filing a flight protocol or registering an approved destination. He had seized the flight school's Sandor Gamma, a reckless craft that should take him far away before any authorities could catch up with him.

He knew the Humans and that Mantrin weapons specialist had ruined his plans again—but those three had departed days before, too long ago to have caused all this new trouble. Golbus had no idea how the authorities had tracked him down. Who had exposed him?

Never before had he let himself be bothered by the criminal sentences and arrest warrants waiting for him on twelve other systems. Fauldro would merely be the thirteenth—yet he couldn't understand what had gone wrong so quickly.

Gripping the piloting controls with his top set of hands, he left Fauldro's atmosphere and accelerated into deep space, heading for planets he had never before visited out on the edge of the Spiral Arm. The Sandor Gamma was certainly fast, with engines roaring so hard the whole craft vibrated as if he were passing through an ion storm. Steering was a bit problematic on the too-powerful spacecraft, but as long as he flew in a straight line—straight *away* from Fauldro—he had nothing to fear.

Some time later, Golbus emerged near a system whose name he didn't recognize, a mere blip on the charts. He hoped he could make a fresh start here, far from any troublesome records. Eventually he would send for his distributed wealth and loyal lieutenants so that he could rebuild his empire. He'd been to enough different worlds to know that there were always opportunities for criminal activities, always fools who wanted to be bilked out of their money, and other fools ready to help Golbus do it.

It might take a while here, but he could certainly meet the challenge.

As he came around the world's edge, Golbus's scanners detected the engine signatures of several ships. Ah, so at least this was a civilized society. Whoever lived here had spacefaring capabilities, and Golbus was sure he had something to offer them. Even without seeing or identifying the alien race, he began to make plans.

He cruised in a fast, low orbit, emerging from the night shadow of the planet. But upon opening his hailing frequencies to contact the ships, automatically broadcasting signals of peace, he felt as if he had fallen into a nightmare. An all-too-familiar nightmare.

Instead of finding friendly spacecraft or even neutral vessels from another galactic commercial empire, he saw several glowing blue ships. Drej Stingers!

The crablike, angular vessels that had haunted him for years.

With a muttered oath, Golbus reversed his thrusters. But when he tried to steer, the Sandor Gamma responded clumsily, heading off at an angle from where he had intended to go.

The Drej scout ships experienced no such difficulty. Pulsing with eerie energy, they accelerated in perfect unison as if the aliens themselves shared a single mind. Perhaps that was indeed the case.

"No!" Golbus cried, punching control buttons, searching for the weapons banks.

But the insectlike ships surrounded him, firing upon his engines with power-draining plasma bursts. His ship stuttered, trying to flee, but losing ground every second.

Then, with a deadly glow like a hot blue sun, a much larger vessel came from behind the Stingers, looming up over the edge of the planet below. Though already huge, it kept getting bigger.

Golbus thought of all the horrors he had heard about the Drej, not just how they blew up civilizations, but how they viewed other species as subjects for interrogation or experimentation . . . perhaps even food. Nobody knew. The Drej were mysterious. Lightning flowed through their veins instead of blood.

Whimpering, Golbus fired a big burst from his thrusters and flew straight forward, ramming into one of the Drej ships. But the alien vessel was already *dissolving*, folding itself into a linkup with the other ships, joining to form a larger cluster.

Sparks flew from the Sandor Gamma's control panels. One of his engine pods flared and burned out, sending the ship spinning out of control.

Instead of crashing through the alien blockade, Golbus found himself stuck like a panther beetle in a droplet of blue jelly. No matter how he fired the Sandor Gamma's remaining engines or tried to power up the academy ship's weapons systems, he could not strike back. He could not break free.

"No, no!" he shouted.

Then he heard the blue-fire aliens banging against his hull. Trying to get in.

After a few moments, the metal hatch glowed orange, then red. The Drej cut through the solid bulkhead and let the smoking slab crash onto the deck. Golbus crawled into a back corner, flailing all four of his arms, trying to make the aliens go away.

Drej drones stepped onto the red-hot metal without feeling the heat. They simply absorbed the energy as they strode forward, angular arms and long fingers outstretched to grab him.

Golbus kicked and punched, but his blows were ineffective against the pulsing aliens. It took four of them to drag him out of the captured spacecraft. But in the end, they succeeded in bringing the Solbrecht crime lord into their glowing Mothership.

The Drej already had one of their best interrogation chambers prepped and ready for their latest victim. . . .

— 24 —
EPILOGUE

"It sure feels good to be flying the *Ronin* again," Akima said, making calculations for the flight protocol that would take them from Qu'ut Minor to Houston colony.

"Yeah. Awful nice of Dhornan to fly this hunk of junk off of Fauldro and meet us in the cometary cloud. That was a good idea you had." Stith lounged back in the copilot seat, which had been modified to accommodate her Mantrin bulk. "But I never realized you two were so close at the academy."

"Neither did I, but Dhornan wasn't the type to make *friends* with anyone," Akima said, looking out at the starfield ahead of her, enjoying the feeling of being in open space again, though she already missed Ishaq. "At first I thought he was just my toughest competition for high scores, but in the end Dhornan showed me that even though we're from different species, wc have more in common than I ever knew."

Stith grunted. "Having the Drej destroy your respective homeworlds can really bring two people together, I suppose."

Akima remembered what she had seen on the surviving planet, Qu'ut Minor. "Yes, but the Qu'utians have already rebuilt so much beneath the surface of their ruined planet. It's a bit discouraging that they still have to hide from the Drej, though."

"Dhornan took a big risk to help you—and Ishaq—you know." Stith herself had seen the wary glances from the other ethereal aliens in their hidden city.

"I know. The Qu'utians didn't have to agree to keep Earth's cultural treasures hidden on Qu'ut Minor until we Humans can get our act together again. Right now we're just . . . *adrift*."

"Your time'll come, Akima," Stith said. "The Qu'utians have had decades longer to pull themselves back together than Humans have."

"Sure. And we're all counting on Ishaq . . ." Akima's voice trailed off.

"I know. You miss the kid. So do I. But Ishaq made his choice to stay with the treasures, and we have to honor that."

Akima looked on the bright side. "Of course. Anyway, it's not like we won't be seeing him every now and then. After all, we promised Dhornan and the other Qu'utians to help them get supplies. It really is amazing how much they've done for themselves, all without anyone knowing."

"You're one to talk, Akima. Look at all you've accomplished in a short time," Stith observed. "Learned to be a top-notch pilot, saved Earth's cultural heritage, made contacts with other people who hate the Drej. Not a bad start, I'd say."

Akima sat back, thinking of what she had promised her grandmother so long ago. "I can't let myself pass up a chance to do something worthwhile."

"And right now we're going to Houston colony," Stith said. "Set up our own shipping business, and keep our ears open for anyone who was involved with the Titan Project. That way we might be able to help Humans come together and make a new start." She waited a moment. "Uh, ready when you are, Captain."

"Right." Akima punched up the engines. "Houston colony, here we come."

Akima's skill at piloting, Stith's knowledge of weaponry, and the duo's capabilities at self-defense had become legendary by the time Korso's ship, the *Valkyrie*, docked at Houston colony a few years later. The Human Korso, along with his second-in-command Preed, an Akrennian, and the whimsical scientist Gune, sought out Akima and Stith and offered them a proposition.

The crew of the *Valkyrie* made arrangements to meet Akima and Stith at a Mantrin restaurant in the spaceport sector of Houston colony. Akima and Stith had already ordered drinks before Korso and his contingent arrived. He introduced himself and his friends and asked if they could all sit.

"It's a free colony," Stith said gruffly, and Akima could see that the big weapons specialist was carefully taking the measure of the man and his crew.

"We've met before," Akima said with surprise. "On New Marrakech. You brought me a datacard containing Sam Tucker's last log entry." Except that the last time they had met, she hadn't been so acutely aware of how handsome the captain was.

Korso's face registered confusion, then recognition. "New Marrakech? Yeah! Are you the one who used to work with Mohammed Bourain?"

She nodded, remembering sharply how eager he had been to leave that day. If Korso had only stayed with them, he could have used his ship to rescue Mohammed. . . . But Akima couldn't allow herself to think of that bitter possibility.

"Well, you've certainly grown up!" He looked her up and down.

Preed, the Akrennian, seemed to have more of an interest in Stith. A warning growl sounded low in Stith's throat.

"You said you had a proposition for us, Captain Korso?" Akima said.

"Fine. I'll get down to business, then," Korso said, showing no offense at Akima's direct manner. "I've got some important missions to fly—into some dangerous sectors." He brushed his knuckles on his scuffed uniform blazer. "Now, I'm a fair pilot, but I could use a weapons specialist and a really *good* pilot. From talk among the Drifters, I hear you two are the best."

The odd alien Gune fidgeted and played with a strange gizmo he'd withdrawn from his pocket. "The best, yes! The best!"

Akima considered this. "We already have our own business. What makes you think we'd be interested in teaming up with you?"

"For one thing, the money is good. I'm willing to pay top credits for a couple years of your time. For another thing, it could make a difference in the future of the

Human race. See, I worked on the *Titan* with Sam Tucker." He looked Akima in the eye. "And if you worked for Mohammed Bourain yourself, you know just how important the Titan Project was. I'm going to try to find some of the other people who were involved. And the *map*."

Akima straightened. She and Stith exchanged enthusiastic glances.

"I'm not gonna lie and say that what we're doing is totally safe—or legal," Korso went on. "There could be danger. We might even run into the Drej now and then, but I think you'll agree that all the risks are worth it. So what do you say? Are you two in or out?"

"May be danger," Gune chirped, "but never get lost. See!" He held up the bauble-gadget with a show of triumph, but it fell apart in his spotted hand.

Tapping a finger thoughtfully to her lips, Akima glanced again at Stith, who gave her a slight nod. "We're in," Akima said. "It's nothing we can't handle."

Stith thumped a muscular fist on the table, making squirrelly Gune flinch. "Now, let's talk specifics." Preed gave the female dynamo a wolfish grin of admiration— or perhaps it was something else.

Watching Stith negotiate with Captain Korso and his first mate, Akima knew that she had made the right choice. This new position would definitely not be boring. And it was the most important thing to do. For *now*.

Even before they met, they affected each other's destiny! Get the whole story of their tumultuous formative years. Don't miss *Titan A. E.: Cale's Story*, also in paperback from Ace books.